THE GIRLFRIEND SWEATER

ST BRIGID'S ROMANCE SERIES #1

JENNY PARKER

Thanks to Dine for loving the book, reading it first and calling it "cozy and fluffy".

Thanks to the other writers of cozy and fluffy romances that left me wanting more heartwarming stories.

THE GIRLFRIEND SWEATER

#1 IN THE ST BRIGID'S ROMANCE SERIES

Eva agreed to help her best friend's new yarn shop with free lessons. She's finally starting to make a living as a knitting pattern designer, so she figures it'll count as market research. She doesn't count on the most beautiful woman she's ever met signing up for her class.

Escaping a desk piled high with cases in search of coffee, stressed-out lawyer Katie stumbles across a a flyer for free lessons at a yarn shop. Could this be a way for her to finally relax?

Eva's not sure she's ready for a rebound after her cheating ex, and Katie is far too nervous to ask her gorgeous teacher out.

Yet between tangled yarns and tender touches though, their attraction is undeniable.

Can a shy lawyer stuck learn to knit garter stitch and be brave? Can a bruised heart take the chance and fall in love again?

Find out in the first cosy warm love story in the St Brigid's series, The Girlfriend Sweater.

1

———

Purple desert rose or sunset over the sea? Eva picked them both up and shivered slightly at the smooth slither of the silk yarn. It was completely unfair, she decided, for the shop to get a brand new shipment while she was still waiting to see if her rent cheque cleared. How was she going to survive without at least another couple of skeins, she thought, then resignedly put them back.

She didn't have anywhere to put them anyway; the plastic tubs under her bed frame and the big handmade baskets she'd inherited from her mom were full to the brim with colourful balls of wools, cottons, silks and even the occasional splurge of cashmere when she'd scraped up enough cash. She could always say she needed them for work, she thought, but with three pairs of socks, two sweaters and a scarf on her needles all at the same time, she couldn't even fool herself with that line.

I

She went back to her friend Rachel who was sorting out the rest of the new shipment. "Are you going to help me or keep mooning over those new hand-dyed silks?" asked Rachel with a laugh.

"They're gorgeous," said Eva, settling down to unpack another box. "Volunteering to help you is a special kind of torture for me. Even with your friends discount, your shop is conspiring to take all my cash."

"Why do you think I decided to open a yarn store?" answered Rachel. "It was this or move to a bigger house for my yarn stash." Rachel started popping the new yarns into the little custom-made wooden cubbies that made up one enormous rainbow divider inside the shop. She gave an affectionate pat to the silks that Eva had been stroking. "The woman who makes these lives across the lake on a new alpaca farm. She's going to sell me the roving as well as the yarn and she might do a spinning class during winter."

"Ooh," said Eva. "I've always wanted to learn to spin."

Rachel waved a warning finger at her. "No new hobbies! You made me promise to rein you in. You've got to focus on your knitting, Eva, you're doing so well."

"I pitched another two patterns," Eva said as she tidied up a messy sock yarn display, "and sales are still going well on the Isadora shawl."

The Isadora was her latest creation, a dramatic but simple to construct shawl that become dazzling if you worked in beads. She'd included two different beading designs, one pattern for people just learning how to knit with beads included and another for more experienced knitters who craved a challenge. She loved the idea of a knitter making both as their confidence grew, and from her online reviews, so did the knitters.

"Are you still doing tuition on the side?" Rachel asked, setting out a stack of tiny baby sweater samples with soft organic yarns next to them.

Eva nodded. "Until I can make a full-time living as a knitting designer, tutoring the St Brigid's kids is what keeps me fed."

She actually liked tutoring some of them, especially the shy and snarky kids who reminded her of her own schooldays. She had a knack for helping people figure out tricky things on their own, and there was a quiet joy to seeing a student finally grasp differential equations.

But she was determined, just as Rachel was with her beautiful new shop, to make a success at her own dream. That was definitely designing. To create with numbers and your hands something completely brand new that was wearable art — she loved the highs and even the frustrating lows of designing. It was making a living that was a struggle.

"Well, when do you have time to, you know, go out?" Rachel asked.

Eva eyed Rachel speculatively. "You have someone in mind," she said. "You promised the last blind date would be it!"

"Oh come on," Rachel protested. "You liked Samantha!"

"Sure, she's a nice person, but there were no sparks," Eva said. "I think I'm on a friends-only streak at the moment."

Rachel rolled her eyes. "You mean you're still nursing a broken heart over —"

"Nuh, uh, I don't want to hear it," said Eva firmly. "I'm a proud single woman with plenty going on in my life. I don't have time for romance."

"Who's talking about romance? I'm saying a woman has needs, Eva. Needs!" Eva blushed bright red and Rachel squealed in delight. "Spill, spill!" she cried.

"Portland's only ninety minutes drive from here," said Eva defensively. "I like the bars there."

For a moment she thought Rachel would let it drop but then Rachel's eyes widened. "You mean you're going all the way to Portland for one night stands because Jackie made all the bars here off-limit?"

Eva sighed. "It's just easier, Rachel. It's not like St Brigid's a big enough town for both of us. I never know when I'm going to run into her." Talking about her vivacious and extroverted ex who lived to party always left Eva feeling small and washed-out in comparison.

"You can't let her bully you like this," said Rachel.

"She's not doing it on purpose," said Eva. "She just has more friends."

Rachel tossed her hair back and put her hands on her hips. "What am I, chopped liver?"

"Single friends," said Eva. "I'm glad I got you and Ivy in the split." It hadn't been obvious at first. People had called and texted and messaged, but what could Eva say about walking in on her ex and the cute new bartender from their favourite bar that wouldn't hurt even more? It was easier just to back away and stop wondering who had known before she'd found out.

Easier, but lonelier a year later.

Loneliness felt like a little stone lodged in her chest. Like no matter what she did, no matter how busy she kept her days with work and more work, she was always just a little cold. A little further away from everybody else.

She knew this was just her getting too wrapped up in her own mind, but hell, it felt hard to be positive and believe things would get better when all around her she saw people hanging out with each other, couples walking hand in hand. Families, friends. All the things she'd thought she would have with Jackie, and now they seemed as distant as daydreams.

She looked wistfully at Ivy kissing Rachel hello when she came by the shop with late-night hot chocolates for them. She knew they hadn't had a smooth run getting together, but this now? Smiling at each other like the other person was their whole world, little touches and light kisses like they were just pulled together, closer and warmer? It was like standing in front of an entire cake display with empty pockets and an emptier stomach.

"You know what guys, I'm going to have to call it a night," she said finally. "I have an early morning tutor session tomorrow."

"Wait, Eva, we have something we wanted to ask you. Well, it was Ivy's idea but it's my shop." Rachel practically glowed when she said that. The Stitch was her baby, and already getting steady foot traffic locally, making Rachel's dream of a cozy yarn shop in downtown St Brigid's a reality.

"What?" asked Eva suspiciously. "You've run out of people to set me up with, I thought."

"No, this is a professional thing. I want to start offering knitting lessons, a sort of craft circle for the shop. I was wondering if you'd be willing." Rachel saw Eva hesitate and added quickly, "I can pay you, that's the cool part. There's a town grant for community classes and if I offer a certain percentage of the classes on scholarships, the costs are covered under the grant."

"Why wouldn't you teach it?" Eva asked. "You're a great knitter, Rachel."

"I'm a terrible teacher," Rachel said.

"It's true," Ivy added. "She's wonderful at everything else, but Rachel does not have the patience to teach a whole group of people. Not unless she's willing to lose customers when she loses her temper."

"Plus, hopefully the classes will be big enough that I'll be like your assistant and still have time to run the shop. Please, Eva?"

"Okay, okay!" Eva said with a laugh. "It actually sounds like it'd be kind of fun."

They talked rates and while it was the same amount she made tutoring one kid, the idea of introducing a whole group of new people to knitting was enticing. And she knew that even if Rachel had asked her to do it as a favour, she probably would have said yes anyway. The Stitch was fast becoming a second home to her too.

Walking home that night, back to the third floor apartment she shared with two roommates, Eva felt a little bit more hope. Maybe good things were coming her way. And maybe she could get enough saved up that she could afford the occasional splurge.

And hey, maybe she'd meet some new friends at the knitting circle. Maybe even someone cute.

2

———

"Kathryn!" bellowed out from the corner office. Kate sighed and gathered up her files and balanced her laptop carefully on top. At least he sounded annoyed rather than angry.

"This letter that was sent out last week," her boss, Mr Robertson, said while waving a piece of paper in the air, "they haven't responded yet, have they?"

"We gave them until the 18th of the month to respond, Mr Robertson," she said, dredging up the details from memory. Filing injunctions and evictions was the worst part of her job, and she tried to fudge the dates up a little further when she had the leeway. This one she remembered was for a small pet store that had been late on rent twice. The landlord, one of their bigger clients, apparently had new tenants in mind with higher rentals.

She bit her lip. Law school was supposed to mean getting to bring justice to people, and she'd thought when she opted for a small town professional law office over the big cities, that she would be able to help people who really needed it.

But her boss mostly cared about getting paid, not what the community wanted.

"Hmph," grunted Robertson. "Should've given them till the 11th, plenty of time."

"Yes, Mr Robertson," Katie said resignedly.

"Alright, now there's a new property deal with the Boxton Brothers, possible Walmart coming to town and they want to secure all the rights to this parcel of land," her boss was saying. Katie stifled a groan. Part of the reason she'd picked St Brigid's was that the town was a historical gem, a mix of old houses and cozy cottages in a little valley between the mountains and a beautiful lake. No big box buildings and grey strip malls, just miles of pleasant shaded avenues.

She looked at where her boss was pointing on a map. "That's the animal shelter and the dog park," she said in dismay.

"Dog park's under the county, but there are ways around that. It's the animal shelter that needs to be bought out, and so far they're not budging. You'll need to look into them and see what you can find that we can use for leverage."

Katie's shoulders slumped. She tried to rationalise it in her head. Maybe a big box store would be good for the town. Right now they had to drive nearly a whole forty minutes to the next big town for Walmart. Sure. And then the pet shelter people could always find somewhere else to run their operation.

Even in her own mind, she knew it was a weak argument. Mentally, she began composing her resignation letter again, but then she remembered her student loans and swallowed. "I'll see what I can do," she mumbled.

Leaving work that night, Katie was suddenly glad she hadn't driven to work that day. Usually she couldn't wait to escape and get back home and snuggled up with a good book and a glass of wine, but tonight the moon was full. The prospect of a quiet walk home along the pretty streets of St Brigid filled her with a sense of peace.

And nostalgia. If Robertson and his cronies had their way, St Brigid would look like any town. How could they not appreciate strolling under the art nouveau lamps, past the hanging baskets full of spring flowers, and down the pavements with the soft glimmers of shops closing, cafes giving last orders, restaurants with music spilling out from opening doors. She loved the energy and hum of downtown especially, and was glad she hadn't opted for a big empty house out in the suburbs. Instead she had a huge walk-up apartment downtown in a charming old townhouse.

Her stroll had unwound the tension in her shoulders and now she was looking into store windows, noting the cute displays. There was a new shop opened a few blocks down from where she lived, and their window display was still lit up, full of colourful sweaters and scarves. She hovered just out of sight and watched as a couple of women inside wrestled with a pile of cardboard boxes.

One of them laughed and the other reached over and kissed her. Katie smiled. That was another reason she'd moved to St Brigid, one of the friendliest towns around with a thriving LGBTQ bar scene and plenty of people just living their lives.

After growing up too sheltered in a strict household to know why her girl crushes weren't the same as other girls' friendships until she went to college, it was such a relief to live in a town where she could smile and flirt with another woman openly. Not that she had the nerve to, but she liked knowing she could.

She glanced up at the shop's awning. "The Stitch" was written in bold blue cursive across it and inside, Katie could make out colourful piles of yarn and displays of more knitted things. The shop looked warm and inviting, from the plush stools scattered around to the stacks of craft books and even a spinning wheel just like from Sleeping Beauty in one corner.

She was about to walk past when one of the women inside came over to the door and started pasting a large poster up. "Learn To Knit", it said in huge letters at the top. Underneath, there were times listed and Katie found herself dawdling, considering. She would have a reason to leave work a little earlier.

And, Robertson be damned, she was tired of spending all her time buried to her neck in work.

Knitting was supposed to be stress relief, Katie told herself. And if she was still stuck here when winter came, she'd definitely need a warm scarf.

She knocked lightly on the door. The women inside looked up, surprised, and then the one who'd put up the poster came over and cracked open the door. "We're actually closed now," she explained, "but we open tomorrow at 10am."

"The lessons," Katie blurted, suddenly brave. "I was wondering if I could sign up?"

3

Eva woke up to an all-caps text from Rachel that they had their first new student. For the rest of the day, her phone beeped a couple more times as more customers signed up and by evening, Eva had to sit down and actually plan out real classes.

She'd taught a couple of friends how to knit, of course. She'd even tried teaching Jackie once, although that had ended with more giggling and kissing than any successful cast ons. It didn't feel quite so sore, she realised, remembering that. Maybe she really was getting over Jackie.

But teaching her first real class felt the way she had when she'd first hit publish on a real paid pattern. A whole new ballgame. These people were paying for professional teaching and Eva wanted to deliver.

She had learned sitting at her grandmother's feet, almost literally because she loved sitting on a pile of cushions in front of her grandmother's big overstuffed couch, the two of them working on their projects with the TV turned down low. Eva would chatter on about school and friends to her sweet Nana who would lean over and fix her loopy stitches.

She thought of how patient Nana had been. The first thing she'd ever made was a lumpy garter stitch doll's blanket, one side longer than the other and holes big enough for her doll's feet to poke through. But Nana had washed it and treated it like the finest blanket ever made and then put her straight to work knitting a matching pillow.

Adults probably wouldn't want to start on a doll's blanket, Eva thought. Scarves were great but they took a long time when you were new. Washcloths? She frowned. She knew she wanted to do something special, something that would make them see how knitting could make you feel creative and calm, could be a real gift.

Gift, she thought. A gift blanket. She fired up her computer and started searching her favourite knitting websites until she found a few patterns that reminded her of what she'd remembered. Knitted quilt blankets, made of many small squares joined together.

They could make lots of small squares, practicing their new skills, and then they would be joined together to make a blanket as a gift. No matter how wonky the squares, she knew the pet shelter down near the dog park loved knitted blankets for their older dogs and puppies.

Now she'd need to make handouts explaining the blankets and walking them through the first, a garter stitch square. And she'd need a sturdy washable yarn for this, something bulky enough for beginners.

She smiled happily and got up to make another cup of coffee. This was going to be just her kind of project, researching, planning and writing something people could actually use. She even did a little skip on the way to her ancient coffeemaker by the sink.

Looking at her reflection in the side of the kettle, she grinned at herself. Her hair was even wilder than usual, with messy red curls sticking out this way and that. She hadn't attacked her hair with her trusty big bertha hairbrush or any serum, and she had the frizz to show for it. Still, when she looked at herself, she didn't feel not-pretty-enough-for-Jackie, but just herself, Eva. Red hair, a gallon of freckles and a big smile. She'd do nicely, she thought, and stuck out her tongue at her warped reflection in the kettle.

It had been so long since she'd thought that about herself. Maybe the first months of dating only Ben and Jerry in her bedroom had caught up a little, but now she patted her curvy hips appreciatively. She was mostly muscle thanks to biking around town, and the extra padding felt soft and kinda sexy. Maybe she wasn't a bombshell like Jackie with her long legs and smokey dark eyes, but, Eva thought as she stirred her coffee, the ladies in the Portland bars thought she was pretty cute, and today, so did she.

Amazing what a job you loved could do for you, she thought with satisfaction, heading back to her laptop to compare yarns that might work to The Stitch's inventory.

4

K atie eyed the clock on her wall with quiet desperation. Robertson was still going on about a meeting he'd had with the Boxton Brothers. He'd wandered so far off topic that she knew he wasn't going to get to the point in time for her to make tonight's knitting lesson.

Finally, she steeled herself. Yes, she was terrified of being fired but she was starting to feel like Robertson's frequent threats weren't as serious as he made them sound. After all, she did most of the actual work that was billed while he did the schmoozing. Maybe it was time to stand up for herself.

"Mr Robertson, I'm afraid I have an evening appointment," she said when he paused to take a breath.

"What? Appointment?" he barked.

"It's personal," she said firmly. "A woman's thing," she added quickly when she saw him inhale to bluster at her about work ethic.

He went crimson with embarrassment, probably imaging gynaecologists or something else. And knitting, Katie told herself firmly, might not be a woman-only activity, but technically well, she was a woman. And this was her thing.

She found herself packing more work to take home anyway, cursing her own dutifulness but unable to stop herself. Still, she left the office before it was dark and that had to count for something.

She felt almost giddy leaving early. She flung her bags into the backseat of her car and made her way downtown. It took a while to find a parking space but she made it to The Stitch with five minutes to spare.

The little shop was almost crowded. A big leaf fold table had been set up toward the back of the shop, with a quilted tablecloth thrown over it and a half-dozen little gauze bags lined up. Each bag held a skein of yarn and a long cable with little sticks at each end and a small packet filled with mysterious circles and scissors and needles.

The women from the other night spotted Katie hovering uncertainly near the door and came over. "I'm Rachel," she said "and The Stitch is my shop. It's so great to have you here, Kathryn."

"Katie," she said quickly. "Only my boss calls me Kathryn."

"Would you like some coffee or tea, Katie?" Rachel asked and waved a hand at the back of the shop where a coffeepot and teapot stood next to a tray of cookies.

Katie's stomach rumbled and Rachel grinned. "Cookies too?"

"Thanks," said Katie. "I missed lunch with work. Tea would be great."

Settled on one of the chairs with a cup of hot fragrant tea and a plate of little shortbread cookies, Katie studied the other people inside the shop, wondering who would be teaching. Maybe Rachel, the owner? She seemed nice, but she was also busy, going from customer to customer.

Then the little bell at the door rang and Katie had to swallow her tea or choke.

The most beautiful woman she'd ever seen walked in the door. She had fire-red curls pulled back with a simple clip, tumbling over her shoulders. Her face was heart-shaped with an adorable scattering of freckles. She had deep green eyes and pale lashes, and when she smiled, Katie caught her breath at the sweet curve of those pink lips. And her body. Lush curves under a simple sweater and jeans. She was short so that Katie would have to tip back her head when she kissed her, Katie thought dreamily.

Rachel at the counter clapped her hands. "Eva, you're here!" and the woman was hugging her and then coming right over to where Katie was sitting. Katie froze, wondering if she'd been caught staring and then wondering if she should stand up and introduce herself — or if maybe she could just vanish on the spot out of sheer embarrassment.

"I set up the bags like you asked, and there's plenty of coffee and tea. Do you want me to help?" Rachel was asking and the other woman — Eva, Katie thought, she has a name — was chatting back about knitting and guides. All the time, she was standing right next to Katie. Every time she gestured with her hands, her curls bounced, releasing a lovely fruity fragrance.

Rachel spotted Katie sitting still at the table behind them. She put her hand on Eva's shoulder and half turned her towards her. "Hey, this is Katie, the first student to sign up."

Then Eva was holding out her hand and Katie had no choice but to rise up and shake her hand in return.

"I'm so glad you joined up," said Eva. Her voice was a warm drawl. Not a long-term local either, Katie thought before remembering that she was supposed to answer and also let go of Eva's hand.

"I've never knit before," she said, and cringed at the lame statement. But Eva was smiling even wider, her green eyes sparkling.

"You'll love it," she said. "We'll get you started tonight."

SHE DIDN'T LOVE IT. First of all, it was insanely complicated and second, everyone else seemed to just get it. They had got little loops wound round one end of the circular knitting thing and the other end of the yarn wrapped around their fingers like they were drinking tea with the Queen. The woman on her left, super chic with her asymmetrical bob and beautiful floral tattoos peeking out from her off-the-shoulder romper, was already on to her next row.

Whatever that meant. Katie had yarn wound round her fingers and she'd managed to drop more stitches off the needle than get on. She could make a slip-knot, but making more of them with only the pointy-tips of this contraption was impossible.

"Hey, can I help?" The class teacher, Eva, was suddenly standing next to her. Katie's heart skipped a beat and she hoped that the flush on her face was taken for embarrassment.

"Yes, please," she said, offering up the tangle in her hands.

Eva smiled and there was such friendly warmth in her smile that for once, Katie didn't feel clumsy but just — new. It was a nice feeling and she found herself smiling uncertainly back.

Eva took the needles and shook the yarn off, straightening it all into one long smooth loop with a few quick movements of her hands. Then she made a slip knot and another and somehow her needles were clacking along and she had an entire row of tidy little stitches waiting for Katie.

"I've cast on the first row for you. We can work on casting on later. It's definitely more advanced than just knitting. Some of the other people tonight," Eva said, waving her hand at the table of quietly chatting students, "have done a little bit of knitting or crochet before, so it's easier for them."

She leaned in and adjusted Katie's hold on the needles, moving her fingers around with the lightest touch. It doesn't mean anything, Katie told herself, but for a fraction of a second she let herself feel Eva's hand on hers, warm and soft.

"There," said Eva, "much better. Now see, the needle goes through the door - that's the loop on your left hand needle. Imagine it as a tiny doorway and the right hand needle is going in from the front - oh perfect!"

The movements were so awkward and clumsy at first. Picking up the yarn behind was like trying to do brain surgery with a log. Right up until Eva leaned in again and put her hand gently over Katie's and showed her how to twist just so to catch the yarn, her other hand nudged into holding the yarn taut for the catch by Eva's fingers.

Katie barely breathed. When she did, it was that same fruity scent - shampoo? Perfume? Her own overheated senses? as Eva bent closer, her curls falling in a playful abandon over her shoulders.

"Really good," Eva said and Katie managed to nod. Eva's eyes were dark, dark green, she thought. Like moss or old forest. Like what emerald was really supposed to mean.

"Thanks," she said as Eva was stepping away to help another student.

Eva turned back slightly and smiled again. "Anytime," she said.

Somehow Katie got through the rest of the lesson without completely embarrassing herself.

When Eva called time, Katie looked up in surprise from glaring at her hands. Had it really been a whole hour already? She had managed to turn rows and even picked up some of her own dropped stitches by herself after watching Eva demonstrate.

She looked at the little rectangle hanging from her needle and smiled. Sure some of the stitches were bigger and at least two of them, she now saw, had been somehow joined together so her rectangle was more of a parallelogram but it was still fabric. Real fabric that she had made with string and sticks.

"Good job," said Eva walking past her. Katie ducked her head and smiled. She had been the slowest one in the group, but somehow Eva had picked up on Katie not wanting to be spotlighted either. Instead, whenever she'd noticed Katie struggling, Eva had taken up her sample piece at the other end of the table and shown them with clear instructions what to do.

Eva had made handouts for them with clear illustrations of the steps to take. They also included addresses for online videos they could refer to. "Some people learn best in person, some people from writing and others by watching," she said as they were gathering up their things and preparing to leave. "My website and email are at the bottom of the handouts if you have questions. I'll see you next week!"

A couple of the students, the people who'd knit with more confidence than the rest, were already browsing in the baskets of yarn, picking out more skeins.

Katie glanced round the table. There was Milly and Pippa, two older women who were best friends since they were little, they told the group, and had always wanted to knit. Charlie, a guy with a pulled down beanie and plenty of muscles who had held the knitting needles nervously at first and then relaxed. Ruth with the sharp bob who'd sat next to her and turned out to be a natural at knitting.

Everyone at the table seemed to know friends of each other and had chattered enough that Katie's quiet answers to a few questions had gone without remark for once. Katie hadn't felt awkward because she was busy concentrating on her work, not with everyone else lapsing into quiet at a difficult turn or a dropped stitch either.

She folded the handouts up carefully and tucked them away together in her bag with the little bag full of her first five completed rows. She made sure to pull the needles out further out from her little piece and cap them with the squishy plastic thing that Eva had called a needle stopper. Her skein of yarn, an intense shade of blue, still seemed much larger than what she'd knit, but Eva had promised that they'd need more soon and that the yarn store had extras waiting for them.

"I'm going to make a scarf out of this," said Ruth coming up to Katie. "Aren't the colours gorgeous?" She held a handful of something huge and fluffy that seemed to have every possible shade of pink and red on it.

Katie blinked. "It's very bright," she said hesitantly.

"I know!" said Ruth with a huge smile and Katie found herself smiling back. Now she looked, she could see Ruth's outfit included touches of pink from her strappy sneakers, the stripes on her belt to the little rabbit earrings she wore.

"It'll look great on you," she said. "Especially with those bunny earrings."

"Oh great colours, Ruth," said Eva coming up beside them. "I can recommend some beginner one-skein patterns for that if you like." She turned towards Katie and paused, tucking her curls behind one ear. "Katie, I just wanted to say your stitches were good, I mean really good tonight."

Katie bit her lip, unsure what to say. The moment seemed to hold very still, all the other noises in the little shop quieted just while she and Eva looked at each other. She felt herself breathe and words filtering up, a rush of sense-less foolish words about how pretty Eva was, how her hand had felt so right folded gently over hers, was Eva — did Eva like women, did Eva, much more importantly, like Katie?

Flustered, she fiddled with the straps on her bag and ended up just nodding and staring desperately over Ruth's shoulder at the intricately-patterned mittens displayed there.

Ruth and Eva talked a little more, and Katie nodded whenever Eva's glance strayed back at her, but then Eva was moving on.

"Oh wow. You have it bad," said Ruth with a grin when Eva was out of earshot.

"What?" Katie stammered.

Ruth laughed and patted her forearm. "I mean, she's gorgeous. Not my type at all, but I can see the attraction."

"Oh god," said Katie miserably. "Was I that obvious?"

Ruth slipped her hand through Katie's arm and steered her through the shop to the cash register. "No, not really. I mean, maybe?" Katie groaned and Ruth said with sympathy, "I don't think she noticed."

"She was good, I mean at the teaching. I actually knit something," said Katie.

Rachel rang up the sales order. "Did the class go well?" she asked them.

"Fantastic," said Ruth. "We were wondering if Eva teaches any other classes." She elbowed Katie and mouthed "join them" at her.

Rachel shook her head regretfully. "No, this is her first craft class. Eva does design knitwear though." She pointed behind her at a cute flower-patterned tank and a cozy cabled wrap. "These are two of her designs."

"She's not going to expect us to make those?" asked Katie nervously.

Rachel shook her head reassuringly. "No, those are definitely advanced patterns. But if you keep at it, one day you'll be able to make something like those."

At the door, Ruth pulled out her phone and she and Katie exchanged numbers. "We could have coffee before the next lesson," Katie said before she could stop herself with doubts.

Overstepped, the little voice in her head said. She was just being polite, that's all. Who'd want to have —

"Sure, that'd be great," said Ruth. "We're going to need coffee for the next lesson, I was barely keeping up."

Katie found herself responding with an easy laugh, "No, you were great, you knit way ahead of me," and walking side by side to the nearest traffic stop with Ruth chatting as easily as if they were friends.

She waved goodbye to Ruth and crossed the street towards her parked car. It was settling in to a chilly spring night but somehow, she didn't even feel it. Her cheeks felt hot and her chest felt peculiarly light and fizzy, like the opposite of heartburn.

I made a friend, she thought. I might make more. Even the thought of the next day with Robertson glowering at her couldn't dampen her cheer.

And, she thought as she let herself in at home and put the knitting carefully up high where Tomas, her cat, couldn't stalk and destroy it, she could simply look at the teacher after all. Even if she never dared do more than that, it was still kind of a thrill to be around someone who was so gorgeous.

She picked up Tomas, grumpy because his evening dinner was late, and snuggled her face against his soft chest until he forgave her and started rumbling purrs. "I'm going to knit you a cat bed," she promised. Tomas meowed and licked his paws.

5

Eva felt like she had downed half a dozen shots of espresso, she was so wired after teaching her first lesson. She shook her arms and legs out, trying to calm down the leftover nerves from teaching with such confidence.

"You were so awesome," Rachel said, pulling her into a tight hug. "They all told me they liked your class. One of them even asked if you taught anything else!"

"Tea!" said Eva. "I need like camomile tea and biscuits. I forgot to eat dinner - oh wow. This was just - oh wow."

Rachel beamed at her. "You're a natural," she said reassuringly.

She drank her cup of tea while Rachel closed up the shop. Then they had a second cup because Eva realised that she was parched from all the talking. They also made some serious inroads into a packet of chocolate-double-fudge cookies hidden in the back.

Rachel filled her in on all her plans for The Stitch and they commiserated over the struggle to keep everything going in a new business. Eva showed off some of the sketches she'd made for a new project she was working on, a sweater that would capture some of the view of the lake she had if she stood on tip-toes and leaned way out of her window. She wanted to come up with a fair-isle in the same misty blues and dark green forest, paired with narrow cables to shape the curves.

"I've got some variegated green wools that I think would really make this come alive," said Rachel, tapping the little sketches Eva had drawn. "And I have nine shades of blue in the new Jameison's wool." She saw Eva's face and smiled. "Hey, for the test knit, okay? I'll sell it to you at cost."

"Thank you," said Eva, gratefully. "And thanks again for the chance to teach. I love tutoring but teaching a whole group how to knit was so much more fun than I'd anticipated."

"What did you think of the students?" Rachel asked. "One of the older women, Pippa, she came by last week to browse the baby patterns for her grandkids, and we got to talking about learning to knit. Charlie and Ruth found out about the class through Ivy, but the other woman, the one in the business suit, she just walked by last week as we were closing and asked."

Eva took a sip of tea. "She was a pretty good student," she said noncommittally. "Had some trouble at first, but I think she got the hang of it."

Rachel's smile widened. "Oh ho, I know that tone," she crowed. "You thought she was pretty, didn't you! That's your 'I've noticed someone hot' face."

Eva groaned and put down her teacup. "Yes, alright," she admitted. That was the downside of staying close to your college friends when they'd seen you through your first serious crushes and relationships. They knew all your tells.

She looked up at Rachel. "She was really hot, wasn't she?"

Rachel shrugged. "I guess, if you like them tall and skinny. She was kinda quiet though. Did you get any signals off her?"

Eva did like them tall and lean, like they could just wrap themselves around her and spoon her all night long — or do a lot more, her imagination whispered, thinking of the way Katie had concentrated so hard on the knitting, her lips making a little absolutely kissable pout as she did, long brown hair falling in a soft curtain across her face. She shook her head at the question.

"And even if I did think she was interested," she said gloomily, "I'm a teacher. I know it's just a knitting class, but it still feels icky to hit on a student."

"You're both adults," Rachel said. "Well, it's only five more classes to go. Maybe you can ask her out after she finishes."

"I'm not ready to ask anyone out," declared Eva. "Not even someone as pretty as that."

6

———

Katie spent her next three lunch breaks struggling with the knitting. She usually grabbed hot noodles at the tasty Vietnamese pho shop down the block, and for the first time since she'd moved to St Brigid, Mrs Han from behind the counter did more than nod her head and pass the steaming bowl over on a tray.

"What's that?" Mrs Han asked, pointing at the little bag on Katie's table. "You crochet?"

"Knitting," said Katie. "I've only just started."

"Let me see?" asked Mrs Han and shyly, Katie brought out the needles and the two new rows she had managed to add on since the first lesson. That had taken watching a video on a near-continuous loop, but she was pretty proud of them.

"You knit two stitches together and drop one," said Mrs Han and she tugged at the yarn before Katie could protest and undid an entire row. Then she slipped all the stitches back on and passed it over to Katie. "Try again."

Blushing bright red with mortification, Katie stumbled over the first stitch under Mrs Han's firm gaze. Then she remembered what Eva had said about holding the needles so they pulled just so against each other to make enough tension to pick up the loop. Biting her lip, she made it slowly through the next and the next.

"Hold your hand up a little," instructed Mrs Han. "Fingers like that." She showed Katie her own hand, fourth finger bent in a curve and tapped it. "Wrap around there instead."

It wasn't how Eva had shown her, and Katie hesitated. Then she tried the new method under Mrs Han's expectant gaze. To her surprise, the yarn held more easily, sliding smoothly into place. She flexed her hands and did the next stitch and found she was knitting through the loops, her other thumb feeding new stitches on the row with almost practiced ease until she was at the end of the row.

Mrs Han inspected it. "Good," she said. "Next time you come here, I will show you my knitting."

"Um, thank you?" said Katie and Mrs Han nodded and went back to the kitchen, leaving her to her noodles and knitting.

She wondered if that was what Eva had meant by the friendliness of knitting. She'd seen Mrs Han smiling and chatting to some customers, and always wondered what it took to become a regular besides turning up every other lunch break for the delicious broth.

Apparently it could be as simple as yarn and needles.

———

BACK AT THE OFFICE, her day went by quickly. Katie found herself almost relaxed, even with Mr Robertson yelling on the phone loud enough to be heard through the thin partitions between their offices. Apparently, the dog shelter had a solid lease and enough supporters on the city council to make an easy take-over of the land impossible.

Mr Robertson came barrelling out of his office on the way to one of his dinner meetings. Katie who'd been dragged along on these in the beginning before Robertson realised she was too shy to do anything but be a wallflower, bet it was the strip club with the endless buffet this time. She'd actually enjoyed the strip club in a way, although the music had been far too loud and the company that night had been more obnoxious cronies of Robertson. The women had been extremely athletic.

"Go track down the last owners of that land and see if you can find a reason to get them evicted," said Robertson, dropping another bulging file on her desk. "See if they've ever had a citation or anything we can claim for eminent domain."

"Doesn't the city do that?" asked Rachel.

"The council will vote where the Boxton Brothers tell them to vote," said Robertson breezily. "I expect to see some options by this Friday."

When she heard the front office door slam shut, Katie groaned and put her head down on her desk. She really wanted to quit this job but the thought of her student loans was terrifying. The thought of looking for another job, especially one where she would be forced to schmooze with clients all day long was even more daunting. Robertson was awful for a lot of reasons but he seemed to regard her as his in-office workhorse rather than demanding she get out and pull in clients or do the other glad-handling required.

She missed law school some days. The sheer joy of actually practicing the law, of knowing what was expected and delivering it.

Family law in a small practice had seemed like the obvious choice; she loved the thought of actually being able to help real people and getting to do all kinds of different legal questions instead of being stuck in a single highly specialised field. But Robertson had turned out not to be the genial man-of-the-people he'd seemed in her first interviews.

Still, she told herself firmly as she got up to make another cup of coffee for another late night, she was lucky. Lucky to have a job, a great place that allowed cats, and a town she hoped she might come to see as home.

Standing by the office windows, she pulled down the blinds a little to peek out. She might not like Robertson but she loved his office, a ramshackle collection of old furniture and filing cabinets stuffed into a few rooms. It was utterly charming, from the antique glass fixtures that wobbled if you pulled the cord too hard to the big billowy curtains that filled the bay windows. She loved looking out at the wrought-iron balconies opposite with their collections of flowers and herbs on the other townhouses that made up the historic downtown of St Brigid. It was such a mishmash of different architectural periods but somehow, because they all used the mellow creamy limestone from the local quarries, they combined into something peaceful.

She wondered if she could spot the building with The Stitch in it.

She opened the window and leaned out, letting the cool spring air rush over her from the overheated office. The air had the promise of cool rain to come and she turned her face up to the moon hanging overhead and took in a deep breath.

There, behind the next row of houses, she could see the little chimney-studded roof with the red tiles that she thought was The Stitch's building. She couldn't see from here if the lights were on, at least not on the first floor where the shop was.

She flushed, feeling foolishly caught out by her own daydreams. It had been only one knitting lesson, and the woman probably didn't even remember her outside of class.

Still, she thought, leaning on the windowsill, it was nice sometimes to dream of red hair and green eyes and lush sweet kisses.

RUTH WAS ALREADY at a table in the cafe when Katie rushed in. She'd slipped out while Mr Robertson was on the phone, leaving a note on her desk. Cowardly maybe, but the sheer relief of not having to explain again why she wasn't working another twelve hour day was worth it.

"I've got a pour over coming," said Ruth. "Do you know what you want?"

"Double espresso mocha thanks," said Katie.

Ruth's eyes widened and then she grinned. "Add one of their chocolate chip marshmallow cookies on the side. You'll think you died and went to chocolate heaven."

Katie did just that and let out an appreciative moan when she bit in to the warm gooey goodness of the cookie. This made up for working through lunch, she thought.

She and Ruth chatted first about how they'd found out about the class. Ruth turned out to be a friend of the owner's wife, Ivy, from teaching at the art school over at St Brigid's College.

"I thought you'd be one of the local artists," said Katie after a while. Today Ruth had on a perfectly matching blue pantsuit with shiny electric blue heels and a teal scarf thrown casually around her neck in a way Katie was sure she'd accidentally strangle herself if she had tried it. Even her fingernails were shades of blue with tiny clouds painted on them.

"I do some work in sculpture when I can find time," said Ruth. "But mainly I teach life drawing. There are some introductory classes for adults if you're interested. Although I don't think any of our art teachers will match up to our knitting teacher," she added, her eyes dancing.

Ruth was, Katie realised, just gently teasing her and not making fun of her. She stuck her tongue out at Ruth daringly and skipped over the topic of Eva. "This is the first class I've taken since I graduated," she said. "I just needed something to get my head out of work."

Ruth nodded. "I'm hoping working with my hands in a different way will help me too. It's a chance to play with colour and materials that's new to me."

Then Katie found herself asking about what Ruth made and to her surprise, agreeing to attend an art opening the next week. Ruth had lived in St Brigid for most of her life. "I never really got the whole big city thing," she said thoughtfully. "I've always loved the landscape here and the people. St Brigid is home, you know."

"I've only just moved here a few months ago," Katie said. "I'm still trying to figure out if this is home." Then she glanced at her watch. "We've got five minutes to get to class."

Ruth put out her hand. "Hang on, we haven't even gotten to the most important part of coffee — Eva. Do you want to ask her out?"

Katie didn't know what to say. Of course she did, but she didn't even know if Eva liked women, or if Eva liked her. And to ask someone out took her weeks to work up the nerve. At law school, all of her previous girlfriends had taken pity on her shy awkward flirting and eventually asked her out first.

Ruth studied Katie's face. "So you're shy," she said matter-of-factly. "Well, I knew Eva's last girlfriend, and she was a real piece of work. You're different," she said. "In a good way! I think the two of you would be great together, and I'm always right about matchmaking."

"Ruth, I barely know her," protested Katie. "And she's the teacher. It would be so awkward if I asked her out and she said no."

Ruth shrugged. "Then wait until the end of class. Doesn't mean you can't flirt a little. You're both adults, and this is just a knitting class."

Flustered, Katie got up, grabbing her bag and leaving behind enough for the two coffees and a generous tip.

"My treat next time," said Ruth firmly and Katie felt a little warmer at the thought that there would be a next time to hang out with a new friend. Maybe she'd embarrass herself at the class with her hopeless crush, but it would still be worth it if she and Ruth became friends.

7

———

Eva nervously straightened the handouts for this week's lesson on the table. She wanted the class to go well, not just for Rachel but herself. This could be something she could see doing regularly, maybe even taking it to the local schools or St Brigid's College as an extension class. She'd spent the week in-between lessons looking up other knitting instructors and watching some of their classes to figure out how she could improve.

Charlie came in early, wanting to run a blanket pattern past her. She was able to reassure him that by the end of the six weeks, it would be a piece of cake, as it was a simple lace pattern that she could help him through.

Then it was Milly and Peggy nodding hello and finally Ruth and Katie through the doors together. Eva couldn't help but feel her heart sink a little at Ruth and Katie together, laughing. She knew Ruth mostly dated men but the occasional woman too. Together, they made a striking pair, Ruth in her flamboyance and Katie, severe

38

and elegant in a business suit, her long legs sliding in and out of the tight pencil skirt she was wearing.

She told herself firmly to focus. She was the teacher and Katie was a student, and whoever Katie decided to date was her business, not Eva's. *Not even if you wanted to be?* a small voice whispered.

Class went just as well as the first week. She was introducing them to increases and decreases. They all got the hang of it quickly except for Katie who kept dropping her increases somehow back into one stitch.

Katie held up her knitting with dismay. "I've done it again, sorry, Eva," she said.

Eva didn't mind at all. Not if it meant she could lean down next to Katie and take her hands — professionally of course — and show her again how to do the stitch. Katie's generous mouth curved in such a delighted smile every time she did manage the increase that Eva found she almost couldn't look away.

Ruth apparently noticed too because she winked right at Eva. Eva knew her tell-tale blushes were showing but she hoped no-one, except Ruth and Rachel who was watching with amusement from behind the counter, would know why.

Katie definitely didn't, bent industriously over her needles and counting off the stitches under her breath as she worked.

The lesson was quieter this time but at the end, Charlie and Ruth started to talk about the projects they were planning, and Rachel, bless her, came over with cups of coffee to go all round and a plate of biscuits. It felt a little more like a gathering of friends than a class ending. Even Katie lingered.

Peggy had come in too with a print-out of a pattern she was hoping to make, a baby sweater in simple stockinette with a garter border. Eva read through the instructions carefully. "You'll be able to do this by the time we finish classes next month," she reassured her. "It's a pretty simple pattern, and I'd be happy to show you how to seam up the sleeves when you're done."

"My first sweater," said Peggy. "My daughter's having twins so I need something fast I can do twice before the babies outgrow them."

"Baby clothes are a great first project before you start an actual sweater," Eva said.

Ruth looked over at the pattern. "Could I just size this up? Like you said using thicker wool? The guy I'm seeing would look cute in a simple sweater like this."

"Oh no," said Rachel and Eva together, "nope."

"It's proportioned for a baby," said Eva, "and more than that, there's the boyfriend sweater curse."

The others laughed but Rachel and Eva nodded seriously. "It's true," said Rachel. "I've seen it happen to other knitters."

"You make a sweater for someone you're not married or at least engaged to, and when you finish it, they break up with you," Eva explained. "Happens over and over."

"I was going to make him a sweater for Christmas!" said Ruth.

"Stick to a scarf first," advised Rachel. "If he asks you for a sweater next, that's a good sign."

Katie was laughing a little at the joshing about boyfriend sweaters. Eva let herself admire the way Katie's hair fell back in a long shiny fall over her shoulders when she raised her chin and laughed.

Eva hadn't looked at anyone with this much interest since she'd first spotted Jackie at the party years ago. That had been instant lust, electric heat at the intensity in Jackie's eyes as she stalked over from the other side of the bar and introduced herself.

Instead, she felt that being around Katie was making her feel loopy, a little drunk or even a little high. Something about this woman made her feel lighter and easier. She wanted to hear Katie laugh, see her smile. Have her lean over her with that lovely hair swinging down to shield them from the world as they exchanged long lazy kisses in bed on quiet mornings.

She glanced over at Rachel who gave her a small encouraging nod. Then she took a deep breath and went over to Katie.

"I noticed you were holding the yarn differently this lesson."

"Oh," said Katie, "am I doing it wrong?"

"No, not at all," Eva reassured her. "It's just a slightly different hold. If it works better for you, then that's great. There's a couple of other ways to hold the yarn that can work better than the traditional continental for some people. Can I show you?"

When Katie nodded, she pulled up a chair and sat down next to Katie. She pulled out the yarn and the little rectangle Katie had been working on — now with drastically leaning sides — and and placed the circular needle into Katie's hands.

"This'd probably be easier if I could stand here," she said and stood just behind Katie's shoulder. It was easier to reach around and gently fold Katie's fingers onto the needle in the right position, but it was also an excuse to lean in. She held her breath, careful not to let their bodies brush.

It was Katie who leaned back a little, tucking her head against Eva's shoulder so she could see what Eva was doing with the yarn on her left hand. "Like that," Katie murmured, and she leaned slightly further back so that she and Eva were almost cheek to cheek.

Eva breathed out slowly to force her racing heart to steady. This close up, Katie smelled of chocolate and coffee, with underneath the faintest scent of fresh soap and warm skin. Where their hands touched, Eva thought she could almost feel the same racing pulse in Katie as hers. Yet Katie looked absolutely calm, concentrating on the stitches she was carefully making with the new movements under Eva's guidance.

"Good," Eva said and it came out as a throaty whisper. "Really good." She was only half talking about the little loops unsteadily forming on the needles.

"I think I prefer the other way," said Katie. She turned her head suddenly and Eva was looking directly into her dark brown eyes, seeing the little flecks of amber in them. She wondered if her own eyes were just as dilated with desire.

"The other way's good too," Eva said. They were nose to nose. The distance between their mouths were so close, she could feel the sweet breath from Katie's lips.

It took Rachel loudly folding together the chairs to knock them back into reality. The reality which was that she and Katie had gotten far too close far too quickly for Eva to act professionally.

She winced, feeling an apology bubble up in her throat. But it was Katie who grabbed her things and stuffed them into her bag whispering "Sorry" and fleeing first.

Leaving Eva with an ache of desire and the over-whelming feeling of being a complete idiot with a near stranger.

"You've got it bad," Rachel observed from where she was stacking dishes.

Eva heaved a deep breath and started wiping down the table. "Fine, okay, I've got it bad," she grumbled. "Did Miss Tall, Dark and Handsome have to turn out to be a student?"

Rachel shook her head. "You're both adults. Ask her out. She's into you, I'm telling you."

Eva stared at the door where Katie had disappeared into the night. She knew Rachel was right. The only question was when. Could she wait another four lessons?

8

Katie didn't know how she made it through the entire week without handing in her notice. Robertson was crowing because she'd found a long neglected set of bylaws on building codes that no-one had actually put into place. He was planning to use them as a technicality to get the dog shelter heavily fined. "It'll be cheaper for them to move," he gloated, flipping through the list of regulations.

"But if these get applied anywhere else, they'll end up costing other businesses thousands of dollars," Katie said anxiously. "Some of those businesses are our customers too. And the town council can always vote to rescind them because they're really not in the spirit of the —"

"Oh don't worry your pretty little head, Kathryn. The city council knows which side its bread is buttered on. The Boxton Brothers can always use a few more leases if other businesses can't handle the heat either. And that's what we're here for, making a profit for our clients."

Katie curled her hands into fists out of sight under the desk. "Mr Robertson, what about the vet's clinic on Swansea Drive? They're our clients too, even if they're not as big as the Boxton Brothers."

He waved a hand carelessly at her. "Small fry. With the Boxton Brothers, I've got a chance to take Robertson Consultancy to the next level," he said. "No more boring family disputes but some real commercial law."

Katie could tell he was lost in his own daydreams of more money and more prestige. She buried herself back in her work and tried not to think about all the people in the town who could potentially be affected by Robertson's dealings. Especially, not about the dogs and cats who would lose their only shelter.

"YOU WORK WHERE?" she said in dismay.

The others at the table turned and looked at her in surprise. Katie hadn't meant to speak aloud but the question had just escaped when Charlie started talking about the St Brigid's Dog Shelter.

"It's over on Old Causeway, near the dog park," he explained. "We were really lucky with the location because it means we've got plenty of room for the dogs to take long walks and get socialised."

Mistaking the look of dismay on her face for interest, he leaned over the table and asked, "Are you interested in volunteering? Or adopting a dog? There are a couple of great dogs that would love living in an apartment."

"I have a cat," she said quickly. "Tomas would not welcome any competition."

Charlie laughed and stretched back in his chair. "We've got cats too. We mostly get dogs, but we've even got two rabbits living in a hutch in the main office now."

The other women at the table began clamouring for photographs and Charlie gamely put his knitting down and pulled out his phone to show them photographs.

Katie kept her head down on her knitting, pretending she was having trouble with the row. She wasn't; now that she'd figured out how to hold the tension of the yarn over her fingers like Mrs Han had shown her, knitting felt like something she'd always known how to do, an easy rhythm. She had grown quickly to look forward to this evening class, and to walking by and simply waving at Rachel through the window. To Mrs Han helping her pick up a lost stitch and showing her a beautiful baby dress she was making. Making her first real possible friend in St Brigid with Ruth.

What would they all think when they found out she was involved in something as despicable as closing down the dog shelter?

Charlie was talking about a litter of puppies someone had brought in and the difficulties of running a no-kill shelter. "We wouldn't be able to make it work," he said, "without all our volunteers and the fact that the lease is incredibly generous."

"That would be Mrs Graham's doing," said Peggy, nodding wisely. "She had a pack of farm dogs from when she lived on that ranch, you remember, Milly. Spoilt them rotten when she retired.

By the time she died, she had about a dozen dogs and no children, so she left the land to the city under the condition that there would be a dog park and some kind of dog shelter."

"You knew her?" said Charlie with interest. "We've got some old photographs of her up in the office, but I've never met anyone who actually knew her."

"Knew of her," said Peggy. "She was old when I was a girl. Used to go around the streets dressed up in her best clothes with a great big walking stick that she'd whack on the pavement and at your feet if you didn't step smart."

Milly laughed. "Oh Peggy, you were always scared of her. I did know her family a little," she said, turning to Charlie. "My mother worked for Mrs Graham's sister, the one that wrote all those books they keep up at the college, about the hot springs and the plants."

Ruth sat up suddenly. "Wait, you're telling me Sarah G. Bird was creepy old Mrs Graham's sister?"

Peggy nodded. "Married a man named Bird. Left him and kept the name. Came back and lived next door to her sister until she died."

"I knew she lived in St Brigid's, but I had no idea they were family," said Ruth. "I've seen the watercolours and the engravings for her books, they're beautiful. She could have been a well-known painter if she'd gotten the recognition she deserved."

"We've got some paintings of dogs by her at the office," said Charlie. "They say Graham at the bottom, not Bird, so I thought they were Mrs Graham's. They're really good."

Ruth clapped her hands. "Oh, I'd love to see them. I did a paper on her when I was a student at St Brigid's College, years ago. When would be a good time to come by, Charlie?"

In her growing anxiety, Katie had dropped two stitches and was trying to pick them up but was instead just laddering further and further down the knitted piece on her needles. She felt the prickle of unshed tears at the back of her eyes and the tightening in her chest that meant soon she would have to make a hurried excuse and leave the room so she could calm down in private.

She hated feeling so weak, and worst of all, knowing she was weak for not being able to stand up for herself or somehow change the subject gracefully. Instead, all she could do was think of those sweet dogs and cats — just like Tomas when she had gotten him from the shelter in San Francisco — facing the move of the shelter, or worst of all, closure.

"Hey," said Eva quietly at her side. "Let me help you with those dropped stitches, okay? There's a neat trick with a crochet hook, look." Eva whipped out what looked like a long skinny bent needle and started picking up a dropped stitch and somehow, miraculously, looping it up quickly back onto Katie's needle.

"You try for the other stitch," offered Eva, holding out the hook.

Katie took a deep breath and took the hook. Their fingers brushed in passing, and although Katie couldn't nerve herself up to looking at Eva's lovely face, just that slight brush of fingers together was electric.

She was much slower than Eva's swift hooking, but the yarn went back on in a lopsided loop finally, and when Eva smoothed down the fabric, it looked as though nothing had ever been wrong.

"Part of why I love knitting," said Eva, still leaning down and talking softly as though they were alone, "is that all your mistakes are fixable."

Fixable, Katie thought, looking at her not-so-little anymore knitting. Maybe she could figure out a way to fix this. She felt a little burst of confidence, seeing how far she'd gotten.

She turned and smiled sincerely at Eva. "Thanks," she said and Eva blushed.

It was a redhead's blush, bright pink rising up from her throat and across her face, the prettiest pink Katie had ever seen. Eva pressed her face to her cheeks and looked even more mortified. "I'm bright red, aren't I?" she said and Katie couldn't resist reaching out for just a moment to brush the back of her fingers against the sweet curve of Eva's cheek.

"Oh, I'm so sorry—" she stammered but Eva's blush was still there along with a shy smile.

"Don't be," said Eva. "I'm not."

Then she was up and walking back to the top of the table to demonstrate a new cast-on method, the blush slowly fading away.

Ruth turned and raised an eyebrow Katie's way, mouthing *what happened*, but Katie just shook her head and concentrated on Eva's hands demonstrating the cable cast on. It was next to impossible because all she could think now wasn't Robertson and her terrible job or even Charlie and the cute puppies but a fevered replay of the way Eva's eyelids had fluttered closed for a moment when Katie had brushed her pink cheek.

She really, really wanted to know how far that blush extended, she thought. And what did Eva mean by "I'm not"?

She snuck a glance up at Eva's face but Eva was all professional teacher now. Katie wondered if she had misinterpreted what Eva meant. Was it a kind brush-off? Or did Eva feel that same magical chemistry between them?

At the end of the lesson, Katie managed to dodge Ruth's questions again but she knew when they met up for the art gallery opening next Friday night, she wouldn't be so lucky.

To Katie's dismay, Eva's wave goodbye was almost polite rather than warm. But then she was busy, chatting with

Milly and Peggy who had questions about casting on for their planned baby sweaters.

She told herself firmly on the walk home to stop daydreaming about her gorgeous knitting instructor and concentrate on the real problem at hand.

How was she going to fix things with the dog shelter? And how would she escape Mr Robertson?

9

———

Eva flung herself onto one of the comfy poufs in the corner of the shop, put her arm dramatically over her eyes and groaned. "I was so unprofessional," she said. "Just fire me now before I manage to make an absolute idiot of myself over that girl."

Rachel laughed and brought out cups of tea. "I bet no-one else noticed your little moment with her," she said reassuringly. "I was watching all of you from behind the counter, and they were busy knitting, not watching you two flirt."

"Was I that obvious?" asked Eva. "She makes me all aswirl when I'm around her."

Rachel looked across her steaming hot cup at her with sudden seriousness. "Would it be that bad," she asked, "if you did go out with her? She seems interested, at least from the way she looks at you like you're a bar of chocolate and she's starving."

"Now I'm hungry," said Eva. "Do you have any more of those good chocolate biscuits?"

"Focus," said Rachel. "Don't try and wriggle out of this. You haven't dated anyone in months since your broke up with Jackie. One night stands from a bar don't count. Maybe a little rebound romance would be good for you."

"I don't know," said Eva. "What if she wants something serious? I'm not ready for serious, not anytime soon."

Rachel shrugged. "You won't know until you talk to her," she said philosophically.

Rachel did have the good chocolate biscuits. When she brought them out, she held them a little out of reach of Eva until she agreed to come with her to Ruth's new art exhibition that Friday.

"She's done some fascinating new work in pottery glazing," said Ruth serenely when Eva asked why she was so interested in going.

10

---

atie wanted to find a solution before the next knitting lesson when she'd have to face Charlie again. And face herself, she thought looking in the mirror that night after brushing her teeth. Her hair was tied up in a messy bun and she had bags under her eyes like the old school days when she was cramming for an upcoming exam.

She was even wearing her comfy school sweatshirt, the one with the holes in the sleeves that meant you could tuck the arm over your frozen fingers in the cold libraries and still hold a pen. She wished she'd been able to knit back then. She would've been bundled up in so many scarves and fingerless mittens.

Back at the dining table, with Tomas keeping her lap warm, she started researching. She had all the research she needed to take down the dog shelter, so surely it was fine ethically to figure out if it was possible to save the shelter? It was sensible opposition research, she told herself.

She frowned and stared out the window at the stars twinkling overhead. The night sky here felt vast and calm, the low glow of the small downtown area not enough to distract from the huge sweep of the mountain that their town nestled in, nor the expanse of open land all around them.

Sometimes she missed her big city life, especially late night food deliveries. That was a small price to pay for getting to live in a place this beautiful though. She sighed, worrying again about having to pack up and move again. Maybe she would wind up back in San Francisco, or maybe she would strike out for another small town and hope she was lucky to find another like St Brigid.

But, she thought back to the problem at hand, there was the question of ethics. Like it or not, the Boxton Brothers were her clients and she was legally bound to do her best by them. She didn't want to compromise on the legal ethics she still believed in, deep down.

She wished she could ask someone she trusted. She thought of her college best friend, Alyssa and almost reached out for her phone to call her, then hesitated. If she called Alyssa, she'd wind up admitting how miserable her job was and Alyssa would give her the same advice all their circle of friends had when she first decided to go rural: come back to San Francisco.

No, she wasn't quite ready to give up on her dreams.

She turned back to the case law tabs open in her browsers, took out a pen and paper and began brainstorming. Maybe she could come up with an alternative to present to them. Maybe she could find a compromise. Maybe, just maybe, she could find some way to make it better.

It was almost two in the morning, and three cups of increasingly strong coffee, when she found something. It wasn't much, but there was a by-law from 1976 on council rulings. Cross-referenced with the lease terms and conditions, she had the merest inkling of a plan.

Now she needed was to find someone in the town who wasn't a crony of Robertson or the Boxton Brothers. Someone who might actually give a damn about the St Brigid's Dog Shelter. Or better yet, find the animal shelter a lawyer who really cared.

And she had to do it all without breaking her professional code of ethics. How?

She swirled the cold coffee in her cup and petted Tomas who had long since stretched himself out on the table next to her in a snooze. What if she quit, she thought suddenly. But then she'd still have a conflict of interest helping the dog shelter, even if she wasn't working anymore for Robertson.

At least she'd be free of him. She sighed and put down her cup. She loved St Brigid but it was looking increasingly certain that she would have to leave the town. Robertson was the only lawyer's office large enough to require a second lawyer in this place and she'd been lucky to find the position.

She thought wistfully of St Brigid's College, but she knew that the woman working as their legal representative, Esme McCullins, was a fixture and there were no open places currently.

No, she decided. She needed to quit and she needed to find a way to help the dog shelter. She'd keep a clear conscience at least.

She thought of Eva and the spark between them. They wouldn't even get a chance to see what might happen. She buried her face against Tomas' warm fuzzy belly. He batted his paw at her head, his purring her only solace in the very early morning.

11

———

The art gallery was just off High Street on Tallapark Lane in a lovely modern building that still managed, thanks to the ubiquitous limestone, to seem in harmony with the older buildings around it.

It was almost magical with big floating ball-lights scattered through the zen-style gardens against giant spiky green plants. Huge open windows led on both sides to the garden and people were mingling everywhere, from jeans and t-shirt-clad students to people in layers of gauzy intricate fabric to chic little party dresses. A real cross-section of St Brigid's lively art communities.

Eva tugged self-consciously at the sweater she was wearing. She wondered if Ruth would think her underdressed, turning up in jeans as well. She practically lived in them and felt uncomfortable in anything in a skirt or even a dress. She'd given those up at soon as she'd left home to embrace flannel and jeans. Comfort over fashion always. But now she was designing her own knitwear, she'd started to notice what other people were wearing too and put her own personal spin on her clothes with hand knits.

Tonight, there was a lot to notice. The brilliant gold embroidery on Ivy's kurta, the clever pleats on the back of a man's reconstructed army jacket, the lacy trim on a trailing skirt. Eva looked down at her own sweater and mentally compared it to theirs.

Maybe it looked like just an off-the-rack sweater, but the cables twined in and out of themselves made a wonderfully complex Celtic knot at the back. She'd designed the saddle-shoulders to show off the broadest braid. The sweater carried the memory of crafting a garment that held meaning in each of its design choices from the creamy thick wool to the hours spent getting the neckband to lie just right. She loved how cozy and comfortable she felt in it.

A woman walked past in a short black leather mini topped with a sparkling slip. She paused at Eva's admiring glance at her legs. "I'm Clara," she said with a smile. "Love the sweater, it's got such a vintage feel."

Rachel's idea of a night out beat staying at home and working, Eva thought happily as she accepted a glass of crisp white wine from a passing waiter.

Rachel found her hovering over a tray of tiny pizzas that had some pretentious name but were mostly really good pepperoni. She pulled her across the room. "Your knitting group's here," she said over her shoulder. Eva paused in shoving another tiny pizza into her mouth and gulped.

"What?" she said, frantically brushing her hands on her jeans and checking her face to see if she had pizza crumbs. The room suddenly felt too warm and crowded.

She could see Ruth's black hair with a new shock of pink highlights through the crowd. There were other people near her, Charlie, Milly, Peggy and - yes, that was Katie, standing quietly to the side and sipping a glass of wine.

"I'm going to kill you," she hissed at Rachel who merely smiled and shoved her over towards the little group.

"Thanks for coming," Ruth was saying to all of them warmly. Eva had gone straight to Ruth's part of the display first thing so she was able to say something half-articulate about the strange little mannikins that Ruth had built out of pottery and glaze, all of them with fat glossy bellies and noodley limbs.

Peggy and Milly were talking excitedly with Ruth about some of the artists they knew who had works in tonight's showing. Charlie knew some of the people at the party from fundraising events for the dog shelter, so he and Rachel started exchanging anecdotes about people they both knew. That left just her and Katie alone in the crowd.

Now that Katie was in front of her, Eva thought she wouldn't notice Clara or any of the other beautiful women present that night.

There was just Katie.

Katie with her hair piled up in a sleek twist, some kind of colour on her eyelids that made them look even bigger and somehow sparklier. Eva didn't do make-up but wow, she appreciated the way Katie used it. The soft shades around her eyes, the high arch of her brows and those kissable full lips. She was stunning, and Eva was stunned, caught on her feet with a wave of desire that almost frightened her.

She'd felt a spark yes, even a little chemistry. Yet watching Katie lean her long elegant body against a wall, ankles crossed so that the cross-over on her dress slid just a tantalising bit open on those legs — that was pure desire Eva admitted to herself.

She wanted to put her hand through that smooth hair twist and pull it down in a glossy slide over her hands as she kissed Katie senseless. She wanted to feel the heat that she knew was buried under that cool exterior. To run her hands inside that dress and untie it, see it fall on the floor and Katie step out of it, naked.

She took a deep grounding breath to control her first impulse and walked over next to Katie.

Katie looked up from her glass and saw her. "Hi," she said softly. The curve on Katie's mouth left the tiniest little dimple at the side.

Eva wondered how she hadn't noticed it before. Maybe Katie hadn't smiled enough in front of her.

"You came too," Eva said, and struggled not to blush again. The lights in the gallery were bright and even with no shadowy spaces. Eva wished that they were dim and low so that she might have an excuse to stand even closer to Katie.

"I did," said Katie. "Ruth invited me last week. Have you seen her pieces?"

They traded small talk, but it was irrelevant. What really mattered was that they were looking at each other. Moving ever so slightly closer.

Katie finished her glass of wine and it was Eva who took it from her, fingers sliding along fingers, the two of them for a moment almost holding the glass together with their hands entangled. Eva put it down on the table behind Katie without breaking eye contact. She couldn't have looked away even if the room had been on fire.

Not with Katie looking at her like that.

"I'm your teacher," she said finally when they'd run out of small things to say and were simply looking at each other intensely. "I think it's unethical of me to ask you out."

"I'll quit," said Katie. "I'll quit tonight."

"I don't want you to have to," said Eva. "You're getting good at knitting."

"Private lessons then," said Katie and she stepped closer, almost between Eva's legs. Their bodies were almost touching.

"Would you like that?" asked Eva breathlessly.

This close, she could see each eyelash on Katie's eyes, the dark sweep of them against her skin. She could feel Katie's breath warm against her cheek when Katie leaned in close and whispered *yes*.

12

──────

They'd both driven there but Katie's place was closer. "I'll walk back tomorrow," said Eva when they were hovering at the front gate of the art gallery. Katie nodded and handed over her slip to the valet waiting for her. They hadn't really looked away from each other the whole time. They fell in step as they walked slowly out of the party, the backs of their fingers brushing against each other in the heated space between them.

It was hard to look away from Eva. Tonight her hair was swept over to the side, showing a strip of soft fuzz from an undercut by the curve of her ears. Katie's fingers ached to touch, to see if the short hairs were as soft as they looked. To push her hands into that sweep of red-gold curls and bring Eva closer.

In the car, she turned the radio off. Eva looked out of the window as Katie drove carefully down the streets towards her townhouse. The light from the street lamps washed over Eva's face, painting her in deep shadows like she had been sketched, an artist's idea of simple beauty, on the seat next to her. Part of Katie was afraid that this was a dream during that short ride back.

But when Eva got out of the car, she looked up at the old building that Katie had grown to love, and the corner of her mouth quirked up, her nose crinkling in pleased delight. "I love this place," Eva said. "I've always wondered who was lucky enough to live here."

Then they were at the second door that led upstairs to Katie's floor, and she could feel Eva one step behind her on the staircase, and then they were sat the door. Every moment felt faster than the next and still drenched in slow waiting, hot and tense.

Tomas mewed from inside and as Katie opened the door, he butted his head out, demanding to be fed. He saw Eva and stepped back a little in confusion. She held her hand out for him to sniff, and he butted his chin against her fingers. She sank down onto her knees and rubbed his chin until he was purring luxuriously and Katie stood still, the keys still in her hand, thinking *I am not dreaming. I am home.*

Then Eva stood up and stepped closer. She reached behind Katie and pushed the front door shut. Then put her arm around Katie's shoulders and pulled her a little closer, the two of them stumbling, then finding their balance. Katie looked down at Eva's upturned face, at the green eyes gone dark and wanting, the mouth slightly parted, waiting.

She kicked off her heels and wrapped herself up in Eva's arms and brought their lips together. The first kiss was meltingly sweet, exploratory. This is your mouth, this is your tongue. These teeth bump mine, now we shift and your lips slide between mine and we fit.

They fit so well, Eva's softness folding lush and inviting against Katie's height. She'd felt awkward before, being taller, being noticed. But now as Eva reached to untie the dress she was wearing, she wanted to be seen. She wanted to see reflected in Eva's gaze the eagerness with which she was stripping her bare.

Her dress fell loose onto the floor. Her bra followed, straps coming down her arms and then she felt her bare breasts pushed up against the sweater Eva was still wearing. Katie didn't mind at all.

There was a new thrill in being nearly naked when Eva was still dressed. The look of intent in Eva's eyes, the hunger in her hands as they caressed her breasts, was deeply satisfying.

Eva bent her head and kissed down the slope of Katie's throat, to her chest, gave each nipple little teasing licks before she cradled Katie's breasts in both hands and brought them close to lavish kisses on them.

"Bed," Katie managed in-between the little thrills of pleasure that Eva was giving. "I have a bed. In the other room."

They got there somehow, stopping to kiss every few steps. Somewhere along the way, near one of the walls, Katie was pinned briefly, her underwear pulled down over her hips, over her thighs in a tangle so that Eva could slip two fingers between and feel how wet Katie already was.

Then they were in Katie's bedroom. She didn't feel embarrassed that she'd left the bed half made or that she had stacks of books unread all around. There was no time for shyness, not with Eva pushing her back on to the bed and going on to her knees between Katie's thighs.

Katie felt wild. She dug her fingers into the mattress, and spread her legs wide. She felt absolutely naked and adored with Eva, still fully dressed, pushing her legs open with eager hands, pressing kisses along the stretch of muscles there, and finally reaching her center.

"You're so beautiful," Eva murmured and then her long clever fingers were spreading Katie open, sliding between the folds and along them in a delicious slow torment. Eva's tongue curled around Katie's clitoris, then licked and sucked. It was maddening, the two cross-rhythms, maddening and gorgeous, driving Katie to distraction.

She drove the heels of her hands into the bed to stop from seizing Eva's head and riding her face. Later, she thought, dazed. Later I'm going to do that. But now, she felt like an instrument being played wildly. Shivers wracked her legs and the sweet steady build of orgasm climbed through her.

"Fuck me," she groaned, and Eva sucked with a harder rhythm, matching the steady thrust of her fingers into Katie and it was glorious, shaking her apart.

Then there were tender kisses on her legs, on the dips by her hips, along the small curve of her belly to the under-side of her breasts. And Katie rolled to bring Eva closer for long lazy kisses. She could taste herself in Eva's mouth.

"Take this off," she said, tugging at the sweater Eva was wearing. "I want you again."

Undressed, Eva was generously rounded and incredibly luscious, her heavy breasts falling against each other when she lay down next to Katie. They felt so good, just lying together, legs sliding together, breasts gently brushing and hands wandering. It started again like that, languid kisses and a slow rocking as they explored each other. Then she had an armful of Eva, and she found that her hair was as wonderful to run her hands through, to spill against Katie's back as Eva rode against her, grinding onto Katie's hand.

Katie asked, "am I doing this right?" anxiously, suddenly unsure of herself. She'd never been quite so forward before with her lovers.

Eva tilted her head back and moaned a little. "Give me your other hand," she said. She drew Katie's fingers to her, showed her how to slide her fingers inside, to bend her thumb and rub just the way Eva wanted. The heat of her inner body was intense, the power of seeing Eva moan and grind against her circling fingers even more intoxicating.

Katie tipped Eva over so that she was underneath, wrapped one of Eva's legs around her waist so she could hike her up to be right where she wanted her, to thrust against her fingers and grind. Eva opened her eyes and grinned back at Katie. "I said you were a quick learner," she said breathlessly and then she closed her eyes and bucked against Katie in her own crashing orgasm.

Then they were sweaty and tangled and both of them smiling so hard, Katie's cheeks ached. "I didn't expect this," she said. Eva yawned and hmm'd against her neck, already falling asleep. Katie kissed the top of Eva's head, marvelling at how good it felt, how right to have Eva folded up in her arms, the warmth and realness of her.

13

———

Eva was not a morning person. When a shrill alarm went off, she felt the comforting warmth in the bed shift and move. Sleepily, she burrowed over to the little pocket of warmth left under the cozy blankets and snuggled her head against the pillow. "Five more minutes," she muttered.

Then a hand smoothed her hair back from her face and a kiss landed lightly on her forehead. "Morning, sleepyhead," came an amused voice and Eva swam back up to awareness, blinking blearily.

There was Katie, wrapped in a pretty patterned robe just short enough that Eva could see the length of her thighs, the hem of the robe riding suggestively higher as Katie kneeled on the bed to give Eva another light kiss, this time on her mouth.

Eva returned the kiss and slipped her hand from under the pillow to the sweet curve of Katie's backside. She found the knot on the robe and undid it, one-handed, feeling quite proud of her dexterity as sleep befuddled as she was.

But the robe parted and there was really no more time to think, not with Katie leaning over her, all small pert breasts with rosy nipples just waiting to be kissed and licked. Katie gave the most delicious gasp and leaned further in. Eva's hands discovered that the robe was the only thing she had been wearing and now there were simply miles of soft skin to caress and stroke.

She pushed back the duvet, and brought Katie down in a tumble. There was something so decadent about morning sex, the sunshine spilling in fresh and cheerful on the sleep-warmed bed. Fluffy pillows behind and under them as Katie, her sleek hair mussed and her face still slightly glittering with last night's make-up, looked debauched and extremely hot as she moaned under Eva's touches.

Sex was slower and almost friendlier this time, the two of them exchanging grins of delight when one found something that made the other arch appreciatively. Soft giggles when Katie tried to run her fingers through Eva's hair and got caught in the mess of bedhead curls. It was the kind of good sex, Eva thought, when you could let yourself just feel. She stretched out under Katie, pink-faced from her orgasm and letting another slowly build from the delicate nibbles and licks Katie lavished on her.

Afterwards, lying flushed and happy together, Eva tried to think of something to say, something witty and clever but all she could come up with was honesty. "I like you," she said. "I really like you."

Katie began to answer but another alarm started beeping on her phone. She sprang out of bed and quickly scooped up the robe from the floor. "I'm going to be so late," she groaned and rushed off to the bathroom, leaving Eva alone in the bed.

Eva knew that Katie was a lawyer, working in a local office. She wasn't sure what kind of law or even what kind of office — Katie hadn't talked much about her work at the knitting lessons.

Now she really thought about it, she didn't know much about Katie at all. She sat up, feeling suddenly a bit awkward in someone else's bedroom. The few one night stands she had in Portland were clear: a great romp in bed and then she'd make the drive back early the next morning, treating herself to a takeaway breakfast to avoid the weirdness of small talk with a stranger she only knew intimately.

She didn't know quite what the protocol was when you knew the person in a work sense too. This, she told herself in dismay, was why there are rules about hooking up where you work.

Would Katie come back to the knitting classes? Was she supposed to ask her out on a date instead, or to just exchange numbers and nod when they saw each other on the streets in St Brigid? Eva groaned. She flirted a damn fine game, but when it came down to it, she'd only seriously dated a few women and never done casual relationships. That had been Jackie's style.

What would Jackie do, she thought suddenly. It seemed a little wrong to be using her no-good lying, cheating ex as a role model, but on the other hand, Jackie had a winning streak with women a mile long. Jackie would know exactly what to do and say. That had been one of the reasons Eva had stayed as long as she had. Well that, and the excellent sex.

Although Katie. Whoo.

Eva looked down at her breasts and saw that there were actual hickies there. They were especially vivid on her pale skin, thanks to whatever Scottish great-something had passed that down with her terrible blushing. She found when she pressed gently on them, they were slightly tender. Tender in a good way, reminding her of how she'd gotten them. She suddenly felt like a teenager again, necking with the cute girl in class in an empty classroom.

Being around Katie made her feel lighter. Like the world was a little brighter and better because Katie was in it. She'd felt lust and then a passionate love for Jackie, but not this giddy almost friendly warmth. This feeling that Katie could just touch her and she would shiver all over happily.

She pulled herself out of her reverie and got out of bed. Her clothes were folded on a small chair between the bed and the window, and she pulled them on quickly. From the window, she could see almost to her part of town, a brisk ten minutes' walk.

She wondered why Katie didn't live in something bigger for a lawyer, like a house out in the suburbs. Maybe she liked the downtown feel of St Brigid's the way Eva did, the eclectic mix of cafes, bookshops and tiny boutiques scattered among little winding lanes and shaded trees. The town still had the relaxed feel of the holiday spa it had once been before it became a college town. Eva had loved it deeply since she'd been a wide-eyed first-year student here.

Coffee was her second thought once she was clothed. Coffee and maybe some breakfast for Katie to eat before she left for work.

In the kitchen, she spotted a frankly intimidating barista-style machine gleaming on the counter. She'd worked at enough cafes herself to know her way around one. Once she located the beans — heavenly that first hit of the smell — and the grinder, she got it all going.

She remembered from the knitting circle that Katie liked hers hot and black. There was skim milk only in the fridge but Eva managed a respectable latte at last for herself.

There wasn't much else in the fridge. Some take-away containers, a lot of yogurt and eggs.

Eva found another bathroom just off the living room and did the best she could with her finger and tooth-paste there. Then she popped back into the bedroom. Jackie would've just gone ahead and made it, but Eva felt weird cooking in someone else's kitchen without permission. She knocked lightly on the bathroom door and Katie called, "it's open."

Inside, Katie was doing something mysterious with a colourful array of little tubes and pots. She smiled at Eva in the mirror. "I'll just be a few minutes more if you need me to hurry. There's another bathroom down from the living room though."

Eva shook her head. "It's not that, I was wondering if you wanted breakfast? I can make eggs."

Katie smiled even wider and Eva felt herself begin to blush under that. She wanted to offer to cook lunch and dinner suddenly. Anything to get that pretty face smiling at her like Eva had done something wonderful.

"I'd love to but I'm going to be late for work if I don't keep moving. I usually just have coffee in the morning anyway."

"I've made you some," Eva said and Katie let out an audible groan of appreciation.

"Thank you."

She wanted to just stay there and watch the rest of this private, intimate ritual. See how Katie, the sleepy pretty girl she'd made love to that morning, collected and groomed herself into the polished lawyer she looked like at knitting class. Watching Katie slick on lipstick, Eva wanted to kiss it off.

"Right," she said. "I should go drink mine."

"Hold on," said Katie, and she crossed the bathroom and very lightly kissed Eva. Then she swept her thumb across Eva's lower lip. "Lipstick," she explained.

Dazed, Eva went back to the kitchen and finished her first cup of coffee and waited for Katie to come out.

There was no awkwardness somehow about the two of them standing in the kitchen, sipping coffees. Katie said it was excellent, and asked how Eva knew to use the machine, and Eva began telling her funny stories of her time as a barista. It was comfortable and cozy and as Katie's phone began to chirp again, over too soon.

"I can leave now," offered Eva. "I've got to pick up my car."

"No, it's fine. The door locks automatically on your way out," said Katie. "Just do me a favour and feed Tomas. His food's supposed to be on an automatic timer but I usually give him a couple of treats in the morning."

Tomas who had gone back to his nap on the sofa after opening an eye at the people rushing back and forth in his apartment, chose that moment to begin weaving between their legs.

"Tonight," Katie said at the door. "Can I see you again?"

"Yes, yes," said Eva and she kissed Katie carefully, minding the lipstick. But Katie must not have minded for she opened her mouth under Eva's and kissed back passionately. They both tasted of toothpaste and coffee, and then just each other.

Then Eva was alone in a near-stranger's apartment, with a cooling cup of coffee and the dizzying sureness that she was falling in love.

14

Katie was at her desk exactly one minute past nine. Robertson hadn't arrived yet, always a relief. She put her bag down and turned on her computer, tidied up a stack of paperwork tossed carelessly over her desk by Robertson the day before after she'd left and then sat there, staring blankly at nothing.

Had she really done that? Had she picked up her knitting instructor, taken her home from an art opening and made love to her — and again this morning! — and just asked her, boldly, like she did this all the time! out for dinner that night?

Yes, she had. She didn't know where she'd gotten the bravery to do it, but she'd done it. And thinking back over the night they'd had together, the way Eva had moved against her, the feeling of her hand caressing Eva's waist, sliding down those generous thighs to the hot — she shook herself and sat up straight. No fantasising at the office. Even when she was alone.

She was glad of that because Robertson came bursting through the door a moment later, ranting at someone on his phone. She nodded politely at him and his glance moved over her like she wasn't even there.

But today, she didn't care. She was too full of some new kind of energy, some kind of screw it and leave it sass that had fired up from the moment she'd gotten out of bed at her alarm and looked down and seen a beautiful woman under the duvet, naked. She'd been bold the night before, and she wanted to be bold now.

She opened her personal email on her phone and scanned through her folders until she came to the email she was looking for. Alyssa Chau, her debate prep partner who'd been patient even when Katie was nervously throwing up in trash bins the moment before they had to present. They'd been close in law school and stayed in touch even though Alyssa stayed in litigation in San Francisco while Katie struck out on her quixotic dream of a small town and family practice.

She paused, wondering what to write. Be bold, she told herself. Ask for what you want.

She wrote quickly, filling in the details as much as she could in a terse list, and including links to the shelter's website and the town's. Then she hit send and put her phone back down again.

It buzzed just as she did, and she picked it up, surprised Alyssa had replied so fast.

But it was Eva, sending a snapshot of her sitting at the kitchen counter with Tomas cradled on her lap, his snub nose lifted in a purr as Eva stroked him. She'd captioned it "I'm being held hostage by your cat. CUL8R."

Katie usually hated text slang but somehow from Eva, it was adorable. She hesitated and quickly hit the heart emoji back, feeling like a shy teenager and a badass woman simultaneously.

Then she looked at her inbox and the barrage of emails sent from Robertson and sighed. He basically just forwarded work on to her now, sometimes not even bothering with more than a deadline at the top. She'd had the naïve idea that he would be a mentor and help her develop into a good family lawyer, like he'd promised in her job interviews. Instead she was mostly drafting up real estate agreements and a seeming never-ending series of letters from jerks shouting at other people. Even the occasional divorces and child custody cases he took were mostly awful, acrimonious and petty.

She sorted through her list of tasks for the day and got to work. If she wanted to leave early two days in a row to meet Eva, she needed to work through lunch. Luckily, she had a stash of snackbars in her drawer for days just like that.

Although, maybe today, she thought. Maybe today she'd just leave. After all, what was the worst Robertson could do? Fire her?

With a smile on her face, Katie got to work.

15

———

Eva walked back to pick up her car, humming under her breath. She might have slunk past The Stitch to avoid being caught by Rachel who would know exactly why Eva's car was still near the art gallery, but her mood was too good to fret about the embarrassing grilling she'd get later on.

She drove back to her apartment and climbed the steps, practically jumping them. Inside her room, she put down her keys in the little handmade pot for them by the door, spun around and fell back on her bed, hugging a pillow to herself.

She wanted to tell someone how wonderful she felt, she realised. And that someone was Katie.

Which was exactly the kind of clingy behaviour that Jackie had hated so much. And it was way too early to be this intense about someone. Eva knew she had a tendency to be super enthusiastic and passionate that overwhelmed people. Rachel and her other friends told her that it was endearing, but it was part of the reason she had ended up trying to build an independent career rather than work in a stifling office.

She enjoyed teaching her students, well almost all of them. And now she knew that she wanted to teach knitting and textiles, to take her math and art history crazy combo degree and do something wonderful with it.

But how was she going to explain that to Katie? How was she going to make someone with an actual grown-up career see her as anything but a never-grown up student?

She was sharing an apartment with two students, PhD candidates from St Brigid's, and she still did the occasional barista shift during the holidays. Would the difference in their careers be an issue? What if Katie wanted someone more conventional?

Eva realised she was planning a whole series of serious conversations with a woman she'd just met, and groaned. There she was, spinning castles out of air when as far as she knew, Katie had only wanted a casual hook-up.

She thought of Katie's lovely apartment, all tastefully picked out in soothing shades of blues and greens. Her very adult kitchen with the professional-level coffee machine and gleaming sets of knives and pans, wine-glasses lined up neatly inside cupboards. Katie even had towels folded into little rolls inside her bathroom.

Eva had a towel flung over the back of a chair and couldn't even keep a cacti alive, let alone a full cat.

Still. She looked at her phone and the little heart Katie had sent in reply. Maybe Katie would want more nights. Before she got to know what a disaster Eva really was.

Maybe, Eva thought hopefully, this could be something real.

16

A lyssa called at precisely 6pm, just when Katie was walking out of the office. Walking very quietly so as not to let Robertson hear her and demand she come back and finish more of his grunt work, but still, leaving on her own time.

"Babe, I haven't heard from you in ages and you're still living in spa town?"

Katie relaxed at the warmth in Alyssa's voice. "It's more of a college town attached to some spas now. The hot springs are supposed to be excellent."

"You've been working too hard to even try them out? Honey, I looked at that website and booked myself a stay immediately."

"You did?" Katie squeaked.

"Listen, when my girl emails me after vanishing for six months into the countryside and she asks for help, I'm there," said Alyssa. "I've got so much vacation time stacked up and your email came at exactly the right moment."

"Oh, Alyssa, thank you," said Katie gratefully. She hadn't realised until hearing Alyssa's voice how much she missed her. And the rest of her little circle in San Francisco. Maybe moving away had been a mistake.

"We miss you," said Alyssa. "But I thought this was going to be your dream, being an old timey Atticus Finch?"

At that, Katie let out a little sob. "Oh, the town's great," she said, "but my boss. Remember Professor Gilligan? He's like that only even more of a chauvinistic pig."

"So quit and find a new place," Alyssa said immediately. "After you do this dog rescue thing."

"I can't," said Katie. "I mean, I can quit I guess, but I need to refer the dog case."

"I had a look through your notes and I know a guy who has some pro bono time waiting," said Alyssa. "I can't promise anything until I corner the rat, but I think he'll do it."

"Rat?" asked Katie.

"Oh, he's a total dick but he's really good at what he does," said Alyssa airily.

"So this is your latest conquest?"

"One of them," said Alyssa with a laugh. "What about you, how are the ladies down in St Brigid? It sounds like some kind of Catholic schoolgirl place."

"The town and the university are named after the castle on the lake," said Katie. "And it's not all schoolgirls. There's, well if you had asked me last week, I'd have said no-one but um."

"Oh, I know that um!" Alyssa said. "Who is she?"

"Eva. We met at a knitting group," Katie admitted.

"Knitting?" laughed Alyssa. "What's next, you'll be canning jam. Is she like, a farmer or something?"

"She teaches knitting," Katie said, a little stiffly.

Alyssa heard the hurt in her voice. "I'm teasing, Katie. I know you have this whole small town thing, and I love you for it. Knitting sounds exactly like you. But you know San Francisco has knitting too?"

Katie sighed. This had been a on-going argument with her and her friends in San Fran. How could she want to leave what they considered one of the very best cities in the world for the virtual wilderness in comparison? While Katie couldn't convince them, she knew that St Brigid was exactly the kind of place she wanted to live in, to settle down in. And maybe that made her boring, but she liked boring sometimes. She liked routine and ordinary town life and domestic things.

Did Eva? Eva seemed so bohemian and creative. She had funny stories of places she'd been and people from all kinds of jobs she'd worked. What on earth would she want with a dull stick-in-the-mud like Katie?

"Hey, seriously, Katie, I've been dying for a long weekend to get away. I've booked a stay at the Okorocks Hot Springs Lodge."

"I've had dinner there," said Katie. "It's spectacular, I promise."

They exchanged travel details and then Alyssa started updating her on the real gossip at her law office. Katie countered with some of the worst stories she had about Robertson until Alyssa promised that she would make sure her guy got looped in to review the dog shelter's case.

"But you know, they may not have a leg to stand on," she said. "I hate to say it, but what you proposed for those Brothers is pretty convincing."

Katie took a deep breath. "I can't say what but it is worth looking into," she said.

Alyssa was silent for a moment. "You found something, didn't you? A loophole. Alright, I'll make sure Dan takes the case."

Katie had just reached her own apartment when she hung up with Alyssa. She leaned her head against her familiar front door and let out a deep down to her toes breath of relief. She had asked for help and she'd gotten it.

Why hadn't she asked earlier, she wondered as she went inside and Tomas trotted up, mewing. Because she'd been scared Alyssa would say no, that her friends would be too busy to help, and that they would have forgotten her.

She picked Tomas up and folded him in her arms, scattering kisses over him as he grumpily tried to swat her chin. "I have friends," she told him very seriously. "And they've got my back."

She thought of Ruth and Charlie and Mrs Han and even Rachel and Peggy and Milly, and kissed Tomas firmly before setting him down. "And I've got friends here," she told herself, smiling.

All this time, she'd been hiding in the office or her apartment, too shy to explore or make friends.

Her phone buzzed and she read the message from Eva, suggesting a little bistro down the road in an hour. When she clasped the phone to her heart, she felt that strange sweet rush of remembered desire and giddy happiness combined. She'd go see Eva and — would they come back to her place again? Go to Eva's? Was she rushing things if they had another night? Was Eva expecting a proper date?

Katie wasn't even sure what a proper date was. All the women she'd slept with had been as sleep-deprived as her in law school, and picked her up so that somehow a few weeks later, they were dating and then later, she'd look up from studying and find out they weren't anymore.

She rushed to her cupboard and started sorting through the clothes that weren't office appropriate. She had cute cigarette pants and a sleek little top she liked, all crisp white cotton, would that be dressy enough for a date?

She freshened up in the bathroom and redid her make-up for a little evening glamour. Her hair had been pulled back in a ponytail all day and when she let it out, she could see the dent left behind, so she quickly wrapped it up again in another velvet tie and studied herself in the mirror. She looked alright, she thought, a little ordinary, but that was the best she could do without going overboard with make-up.

Paired with a nice pair of heels, the outfit had a certain Hepburn-charm to it, she thought. She swapped her studs for a pair of glittering topaz earrings that she hoped brought out something in her brown eyes. She thought of Eva's gorgeous green eyes, and how she made even the simplest clothes look divinely sexy thanks to her voluptuous curves. Then she thought of getting to run her hands over those curves again, and licked her lips.

The bistro was close enough to walk and the spring air was warm that night. Katie strolled past The Stitch and waved at Rachel at the counter. She wondered, her cheeks pinking with slight embarrassment, if Rachel knew about Eva and her already.

And there was Eva. Curls dancing in the slight breeze and her eyes lighting up at the sight of Katie. Eva slipped her hand through Katie's arm and led her inside the bistro. Of course, Eva somehow knew the owner and some of the waitstaff, so they got a little table tucked at the back near a window. Candles were lit on the table and the lights low so Eva looked even more beautiful, all lit up in their glow.

She'd been worried that they might not have much to talk about but it was effortless, as though they were old friends reconnecting after years apart. Maybe it was the third glass of wine with dinner but by the time dessert, a sinfully creamy cheesecake, came to their table, they were giggling together at a funny story about Eva getting chased out of her dorm with a fire extinguisher. Their hands entwined on the table and Katie felt her knees go wobbly with desire when Eva rubbed her thumb in slow sensuous circles on her palm.

"I haven't even asked about your job," Eva said as the table was cleared. "We just started talking! What exactly do you do as a lawyer?"

Katie's good mood went queasy at the thought of discussing her job right now. "It's pretty boring," she prevaricated. "It's family law with Robertson Consultancy."

"I've heard of him," said Eva, her nose wrinkling a little. "He's some kind of local bigshot, right? Ran for city council I thought."

"He lost," Katie said, pushing the last bite of cheesecake around on her plate. "He's still pretty unhappy about that." She thought of forcing a smile but looking across the table at Eva's lovely kind face, she felt brave enough suddenly to say out loud, "I'm thinking of quitting actually."

"Oh," said Eva. "Would you, I mean, what kind of job would you get next?"

"I don't know yet," admitted Katie. "I could probably go back to San Francisco and get a decent job there, but I'm still figuring it out."

Eva's hand was still against her, and then she squeezed Katie's hand and said, "Well, you're here now. Let's get the bill and go back."

Katie smiled, relieved. "My place is just around the corner," she said. "And Tomas really likes you."

"I really like him too," said Eva. "I like his human even more."

17

———————

Eva had tuition lessons right up until a bare half hour before the fifth knitting class, which she was almost grateful for, even with the rush through what little traffic St Brigid had to get to The Stitch. What with jumping from student to student, all of them panicking over the upcoming exams, and calming them down, she hadn't had enough time to get herself in a tizzy over what Katie had said earlier that week.

She was quitting her job. And Eva got the distinct feeling that she would be moving away from St Brigid then. It made sense, St Brigid certainly wasn't a place for fancy law firms.

Maybe she'd move somewhere like Seattle. Seattle had to have plenty of law firms, and it was only a couple of hours drive. She could do that on weekends.

She pulled her car into park and sat there for a moment. She'd only known the woman a couple of weeks. They'd been dating for a week, if that's what you could call seeing each other every spare moment they had outside of work, waking up in each other's arms every night. And here she was thinking, really thinking about San Francisco. This was crazy, she told herself. Your whole life is here in St Brigid. You grew up nearby, you went to college here, you love this town.

This is just a rebound, she told herself firmly. You're getting all dizzy over a beautiful face and you're lonely since Jackie.

But when she walked into the store and saw Katie sitting at the table chatting quietly with Ruth, her heart told her another story. It wasn't the burn of wanting she'd had with Jackie. It was like coming home when she saw Katie look up and smile at just her, that sweet sweet curve of her lips.

Katie looked a little different today, and it took Eva a moment to catch the difference. Her hair, bound up in a sleek chignon that morning, was free, tousled loose over her shoulders. She looked relaxed and happy.

Eva hoped some of that was her and the very good hours they'd spent in bed. She'd only had time for a shower and to throw on jeans and a pullover, but when Katie looked at her, she felt like a million bucks.

She looked around the table, frowning slightly. Charlie was late. Fortunately today was introducing the purl stitch at last and she was sure he'd be able to pick it up even if he was running late.

She set out the knitted samples of ribbing and a few simple patterns on the table and let them play with them. "Today," she announced, "we're going to learn how to do this. Play with the different ribbings and see how stretchy they are in comparison to each other," she instructed.

They were in the thick of trying out the purl stitch — Katie was a little shaky but got it which was fortunate because Eva didn't know how she'd be able to stop from kissing her if she needed a hands-on demonstration, which would be totally unprofessional — when Charlie charged in, looking worn out and angry.

"Sorry I'm late," he said as he slid into the empty chair at the table. "Work's gone absolutely crazy."

"What's wrong?" asked Ruth, her eyes widening with concern. "It's not the little puppies you got last week?"

"Oh no, they're great, weaning from the bottle just fine," said Charlie. "No, it's way worse. We got a letter from some lawyer for a property developer about problems with our lease. They're offering to buy us out. I spent the whole afternoon in a meeting about it, and I hate to say it but they might be right."

He sighed heavily. "It's a disaster for us if we have to move. The leasc is for a token dollar a year to the city council and there's no way we can get such a great place in our budget."

Eva winced. Property prices in St Brigid were pretty good, but you couldn't beat a dollar a year for a lease. She felt awful for Charlie who she knew put his whole self into his work as assistant manager at the shelter. And the cats and dogs! Where would they go if they relocated?

She asked and Charlie put his head in his hands. "We don't know," he said. "If we had to relocate them, I guess we'll find some of the neighbouring shelters, but we've been able to be a no-kill shelter thanks to this lease for so long. I don't know what we'll do."

Rachel came bustling over, concerned at the unhappy buzz around the table. When Eva told her quickly what had happened, her face clouded over. "Oh, Charlie," she said sympathetically. "Let me get some coffee into you first, you look worn out."

She brought out the good cookies too, but no-one had the heart to eat them. Someone mentioned fundraising, and Charlie shrugged. "We already do a lot of fundraising. St Brigid is great, but I don't know if we can get enough for a new property. Definitely not within this lawyer's demands."

Lawyer, Eva thought. Maybe Katie could help. She glanced at Katie who was sitting very still at the other end of the table. "You know, Katie's a lawyer," she said. "Maybe Katie could have a look at the letter and give you some advice?"

Charlie looked up at Katie. "Really? That would be great. I mean, the letter's full of all this stuff about clauses in our lease no-one's looked at for years. We couldn't afford to pay much, Katie, but we'll try."

Katie's shoulders hunched and she didn't look at all eager, or even relaxed. She looked, Eva thought, upset.

"I can't," she said quietly. "I'm so sorry, Charlie, but I can't."

"That's alright," said Charlie. "Not your specialty?"

Katie shook her head. To Eva's alarm, there were tears glinting in her eyes. "It's not that," she said. "I drafted the letter. I work for the property developer's lawyer."

There was absolute quiet at the table. Charlie looked too stunned to speak. It was Ruth who broke the silence. "You work for that asshole?"

Katie nodded. She started packing up her things and stood up hastily. "I shouldn't — I'm so sorry, Charlie." And then she fled.

Ruth looked at the door swinging shut behind her, hurt written over her face. "I can't believe it," she murmured. "She seemed so nice. I really liked her."

So do I, thought Eva. Behind her, she felt Rachel pass by and give her arm a gentle squeeze of sympathy. She was suddenly very grateful they hadn't told anyone else in the knitting circle that they were dating.

Because now she wondered, do I even know Katie at all?

18

———————

Katie had never been so glad for the weekend to come. Robertson was relentlessly crowing about his scheme and the Boxton Brothers themselves descended on the office full of cheer about their new strategy to take Robertson out to celebrate. Robertson didn't mention that the hard work had been Katie's, and for once she was absolutely glad of that. The fewer people who knew what she'd done, she thought as she packed her bag, savagely shoving things in, the better.

She was desperate to leave and to fix things, but she knew what mattered most was the way her new friends had looked at her. Maybe back in San Francisco it would've been just another day at the office, but here in St Brigid everyone knew everyone else. And she had just been starting to put down roots and make real friends when this happened.

She slammed the office door behind her, grateful that Robertson had left early for his Friday nights drinks so that she could leave. There was plenty of work still on her to-do list, but for once she didn't give a damn.

Alyssa was landing that evening and meeting her at the Okorocks Hot Springs Lodge. It was just what she needed, dinner with someone who really knew her and wouldn't judge her until she knew the whole story. And who, she fervently hoped, might have a solution.

Because her phone was still silent. She hadn't dared message anyone else in the knitting class, but she'd sent Eva a note asking if they could meet and talk.

Eva had replied with a short "maybe later. Busy this week."

Katie had stared at the message, crushed. Maybe St Brigid wasn't the right place for her. Maybe this was only a casual fling for the other woman.

But tonight, she told herself, as she swung her car up and down the winding road from town to the Lodge, she would at least get a chance to relax. And the drive up to the Lodge, nestled in the foothills of the Okorocks, was a beautiful drive, winding through patches of old forest and grazing fields with the occasional sheep or even, she'd seen once, alpacas looking quizzically back at her.

The Lodge was almost the oldest building in all of St Brigid after the big house that Widow Bartley had first built along her peculiar castle folly on St Bridgid's Island in the nearby lake. The Lodge was high up enough that you could make out the little turrets on the castle folly in the middle of the lake, a gorgeous view that swept in all the surrounding countryside with St Brigid proper like a tiny dollhouse town.

Alyssa was waiting for her at the Lodge bar, looking impossibly chic in a sweater and pants combo, somehow sleekly tailored and rumpled casual simultaneously. She'd taught Katie how to dress back in law school, teaching her enough that Katie had stopped showing up to class in sweatpants and a baggy t-shirt, but Alyssa always managed to look cutting edge fashionable.

"Darling!" she cried and swung Katie into a bear hug. She barely reached Katie's shoulders but her grip was fierce and Katie returned the hug with the same warmth.

"Now sit out on the terrace. We will drink something fabulous and breathe all this fresh mountain air — the view is as stunning as promised — and you will tell me all about this girl, Eva."

"If you tell me about Dan," Katie said. She was already feeling cheered up, buoyed by Alyssa's enthusiasm on seeing her again. It was like the past few months of misery had vanished with her old best friend back by her side.

Alyssa waved a hand. "Dan is old news. I've got George, Hans and Yihong in rotation now."

Over a fantastic dinner of seared salmon and microgreens, Katie filled Alyssa in on everything that had happened since they'd last seen each other.

It felt so good to finally open up about how bad the situation at work had gotten. Alyssa commiserated, but she was forced to admit that she loved her own job at the law firm, even with the grindingly long hours.

"You're not suited to this," she said finally. They were sipping wine, sitting side by side on a luxuriously padded bench that overlooked the rolling green and blue-hilled countryside.

Katie sighed. "I know. I just don't want to go back to a big law firm yet. I can't think what else to do."

Alyssa regarded her. "In-house counsel? No, you'd have to move to a big city. I've been listening to you this whole time and Katie, you belong here. Or if not here, somewhere else small. You were never a big city girl like the rest of us. Your whole face lights up when you talk about the town, just not work."

"But there are no jobs here," said Katie, frustrated.

Alyssa shrugged. "So commute. Seattle's only a couple of hours away, Portland's even closer. Find a job in another town nearby."

It was so simple when Alyssa said it. Stay here, but work outside.

She pulled out her phone, and Alyssa laughed and pushed it back. "Don't job search drunk," she advised. "Cora did that and ended up emailing her boss a screw-you letter that got her totally fired."

"Oh, I already have my resignation letter written," said Katie. "I think I stuck it out here from sheer stubbornness. I thought if I quit my first job because it was hard, well, that'd be like saying I couldn't hack it at all."

"That's my Katie," smiled Alyssa fondly. "You were always too stubborn for your own good. Sometimes," Alyssa said, sloshing the wine in her glass as she reached over to top up Katie's, "you have to just cut bait and fish. Speaking of which, tell me more about this woman that's got you all fired up."

Katie leaned back on the bench and smiled dreamily up at the brilliant night sky full of stars overhead. She felt like a great weight had been lifted off her shoulders. Then she remembered that Eva still thought she was some kind of evil lawyer who kicked puppies out on the street and she burst into tears.

"Oh, oh," said Alyssa, "oh Katie, don't cry!"

By the time Katie had wiped her face and most of her make-up off with one of the generous napkins the bar staff brought over, along with another bottle of wine, they were both well and truly drunk. Alyssa had convinced her that she would somehow get Eva to understand, "especially," said Alyssa, annunciating every word carefully, "because you, you are so special, Katie. I mean, you're so freaking smart and you like flowers and gardens and farms and all this weird country stuff and this is like, this woman? She sounds totally cool for you. Is the sex really that good?"

"So good," Katie said, slinging her arm around Alyssa. "Oh god, how am I going to drive home? I drank way too much."

"Stay for the weekend, it'll be like old times."

"Alright," agreed Katie. At the hotel's desk, she managed without slurring her words she thought, to let them know she was checking in.

Alyssa leaned over her shoulder and interrupted. "Stay in my room!" cried Alyssa. "We can have breakfast in bed."

The hotel clerk smothered a grin and passed Katie another keycard. "Breakfast is at eight," she said, "but if you like we can delay it until you call the front desk."

Katie could just imagine the hangover they would have and nodded gratefully before heading off to Alyssa's room.

Inside, the king-size bed was massive and there were enough toiletries that they both managed to get their teeth brushed and splash their faces before they admitted they were too drunk for more. Instead, they collapsed, laughing at the huge pile of pillows on the bed for some reason and fell quickly into a deep sleep.

19

———

"Eva!" Rachel said, pulling her into a hug. "I have to talk to you." She had that tone that meant it was bad news, and Eva's stomach clenched.

"Is something wrong with the shop? Or Ivy?"

"No," said Rachel, guiding Eva to a quiet corner at the back of the store. "Look, you've been miserable this week about everything that went down with that woman."

"Katie," said Eva. She picked up a ball of wool and started turning it in her hands, trying to let the warm fuzziness distract her from the stab in her chest that thinking about Katie was. There had been no reply to the last message she'd sent, and the update from Charlie was that the lawyer was a real dirtbag, and that it looked like they would definitely lose the shelter. She wanted to believe better of Katie, but Katie hadn't said anything for the rest of the week.

Would she show up this evening for the last class? Eva wasn't sure. She thought she should swallow her pride and reach out again.

Rachel looked conflicted then took a deep breath and said, "Well, I heard from a friend working at the Lodge that Katie was up there this weekend with another woman. They shared a room."

Eva opened her mouth, then shut it, the hurt like a blow. After a moment, she managed to ask, "Do you know who the woman was?"

Rachel shook her head. "Someone who came in from San Francisco."

So it really was true. Katie was planning to go back to San Francisco and had someone there already. She'd just been a local hook-up, someone to pass time with. Eva's face must've shown some of the hurt she was feeling because Rachel wrapped her up in a tight hug.

"She's not worth crying over," she said firmly.

Eva shook her head. "That's the trouble," she said quietly. "She really is. I was falling for her."

The rest of the class had arrived, and Ruth was coming over, pulling a long length of ribbing from her bag with gusto.

Eva took a deep breath and straightened her shoulders and put on a smile. So she'd had a bad rebound experience with a city girl. It was hardly the end of the world, she told herself. Her heart would mend, and she'd be able to stop thinking about Katie and her big brown eyes soon enough.

No-one else seemed to want to think about Katie either, her empty chair going unremarked. It hurt a little, that Katie could be so easily forgotten but when Rachel had set out the tea and coffee and was bringing over some extra colours of the wool they'd been using in class, Peggy brought her up.

"I liked her," she said. "And it doesn't seem fair to have her quit the class just because she has a bad job."

Milly nodded. "We didn't give her a chance to say her side of the story," she added.

Charlie opened his mouth, anger flushing his face red, "She's working for the property developers who are going to shut down the shelter!"

"Yes," said Peggy, "but they're the ones doing the closure. We didn't really ask her what she thought. There's a difference between a person and a job."

He was quiet for a moment, then slowly nodded. "I want to be fair," he said, "but it's hard."

Ruth nodded vigorously, "I get that, Charlie, I do. I think the closure is terrible but I also can't quite believe that Katie's to blame. Well, not entirely," she added.

Charlie's scowl faded and reluctantly he said, "I guess she should be able to come to class. I don't want to be the kind of person who turns people away because of their job. Not without giving them a fair hearing at least."

Expectantly, they all turned to look at Eva who'd stayed quiet throughout. Her throat was choked tight with emotion. Half of her was grateful for the kindness this little circle of new friends had found, and they were saying some of the same arguments she had been making to herself all week.

But what Rachel had just told her before class stung badly. The thought that what they'd had, that sweet close week where she'd been giddily falling in love, that It had been just casual meaningless sex for Katie — it hurt too badly for her to be generous.

She swallowed and said in a low voice, "It's her choice not to turn up. If she doesn't want to come to the classes, we can always give her a refund."

Ruth looked up from the scarf she was working on and whatever she saw on Eva's face, she closed her lips and looked away.

Eva felt suddenly very tired. "I think I'm going to call it an early night," she told them.

Outside on the footpath, with the warm lit-up interior of The Stitch behind her, Katie looked up at the sky and the distant stars, dark behind the yellow glow of the streetlamp. The night was cold, even in her thick sweater, and she tucked her hands into her pockets, shivering.

She knew it wasn't helpful, but still she glanced down the street towards Katie's townhouse round the corner. She wondered what Katie was doing. If Katie was even thinking of her.

She wiped at her face and set off grimly to her car. Best to just move on.

20

Katie spent most of the week exchanging emails with recruiters in Seattle and firing off applications to every job she could find within a 50-mile radius of St Brigid.

She woke up on Thursday to an unexpected job offer that was forty miles out of town two counties over. The pay was a pretty hefty cut, but she sat down and worked out her expenses and thought she could swing it. Especially with the cushion she'd saved up by being so miserable the past nine months she'd barely bought anything beyond cat food and take-out.

"I accept," she emailed back, and spent all the rest of the day so delighted that even Robertson asked suspiciously what she was so happy about.

Even the sting of Eva's continued silence felt a little more bearable that day. The contract arrived by email that evening. She fired off an email to Alyssa with profuse thanks and then sent her new job details to Dan, who had already gotten in touch with the shelter.

She still didn't feel it was ethical for her to give him any advice about the case, but he'd worked out some of the same strategy she'd spotted and she was confident that he'd be able to get the better of Robertson. He had a gleeful note when he wrote back to tell her he'd keep her updated and that the bastards were going down. Attached was a picture of his own cute bull terrier.

She walked around her apartment on Friday night, marvelling at all the ways she saw now that she'd begun to make this place home. Tomas' enormous cat tower that he liked to climb and pounce down from. A beautiful handwoven blanket on the back of her sofa, a tiny succulent garden on her coffee table. All her books filling up the bookcase that she'd put together herself on a long weekend.

This could be her real home, she thought gratefully. She leaned against her bedroom door and looked at her bed, neatly made with the huge fluffy duvet she'd snuggled under with Eva in her arms. Thinking of Eva made her feel a strange mix of hope and sorrow.

Tomorrow, she promised herself. Tomorrow she would quit and she would message Eva and ask, no beg if she had to, for another chance to talk.

And even if Eva was done with her, Katie thought a little tearfully, it didn't mean she had to give up on everybody. She'd been brave enough to try and set down some roots in St Brigid, and if it hadn't been for awful

Robertson — well, she wasn't going to give up again, she vowed.

The next day the sky was bright and clear, a beautiful late spring day. Katie took especial care with her clothes, opting for things that felt almost like armour. Her lucky pearl earrings, a gift from the aunt who'd helped raise her after her parents had turned chilly when Katie came out in high school. The first real silk piece she'd bought after law school to look like a real lawyer, and her favourite pair of sleek black pumps.

She picked Tomas up for an extra cuddle before she left, even though it meant going over all her clothes again with a lint brush hanging on the coat rack. "We'll celebrate with tuna for you," she promised, and Tomas purred loudly.

Robertson was naturally late to the office, and when he came in, on another loud one-sided conversation on his headset. He pointed at the coffee machine and raised his finger for one, then slammed into his office.

Katie found herself automatically moving to make the coffee when she stopped herself. She didn't have to make him coffee again. She didn't have to do anything for Robertson again.

She knocked on his door and when he grunted, she opened it.

"I quit, Robertson," she said with her chin stuck out to keep her voice from quavering. The man had bullied and belittled her for long enough. She wasn't going to take it any longer.

"You can't quit," said Robertson. "What else are you going to do in this town? I'll make sure you don't get another job!"

"I have one lined up already. I'm going to be a mediator for the local county center," said Katie serenely. She thought of the letter she'd typed up months ago and carried daily in her bag, never daring to take it out. Now it was retyped neatly with today's date and her signature. She held it out to him. "My notice," she said.

He took it dumbly and stood there, his mouth still open. Then he launched into a profanity-laced speech about how he'd make sure she got fired, how he'd make sure everyone in town knew just what kind of a rip-off she'd tried to run on him and the Boxton Brothers…

Katie folded her arms and waited until he'd run out of breath. "Good luck replacing me," she said calmly, picked up her briefcase and walked out the door.

Tomas looked up when she came home surprisingly early, and then fluffed up his fur and ignored her, continuing to stare out of the window at the birds opposite. He was chittering at them, and to her amusement, meowed in annoyance when she came over to nuzzle his head.

"I thought you'd be happy to see me," she scolded him and then went to the kitchen to make a celebratory cup of coffee.

With caffeine buzzing in her system, she felt almost ready to text Eva. She'd done something so enormous just now, she thought, holding her phone carefully like she might slip and accidentally send a string of heart emojis, then how could this be that hard?

Yet it was. She realised then, standing in her kitchen, wired from quitting her first job and landing another, saving a dog shelter and standing in her very own grown-up real apartment that what she wanted wasn't just a great job and a place she loved.

All those years she'd been dreaming of living in a small town, she'd been dreaming of someone next to her. Dreaming of a woman who would love this quiet domestic life, who was funny and smart and creative and beautiful, all the things that Eva was. All the things she'd fallen head over heels in love with. Someone who just by standing there and *looking* at her made her feel brave enough to say the things she wanted. Who made her want to be a better person.

She wanted Eva so much. She wanted to make love to her in the evenings and wake her with kisses in the mornings. She wanted to build a home with her.

Would Eva? Could she explain to Eva well enough that Eva would see who she really was? Was she just a passing fling for Eva? Someone she could let slip away as easily as they'd seemed to come together?

She fidgeted with the keys on her phone and finally unlocked it and began to type.

Dear Eva, she wrote. *Can we meet? I really want to talk.*

21

Eva's phone buzzed in her bag. She ignored it to patiently walk Calvin through the steps in solving his physics homework again. Probably Rachel checking in on her again.

Eva had managed to eat two pints of Ben and Jerry's slumped on her sofa before her own energy kicked in. She had needed to express herself creatively and the result was one of the cuddliest sweaters she could imagine, something with too-long arms that scrunched up and a generous boxy shape that you could huddle down in and pull over your knees to form a little cozy blanket to shut the rest of the world out.

She'd hunted through her stash and dug up some fuzzy cream-wool mohair mix that turned the simple lines of her sweater into a cloud of heavenly softness. Knitting it madly over the last week had been the only thing that had helped her to stop feeling so wretched. She was starting to worry when she'd get round to casting off, because what with knitting it from the top-down, she could already pull it almost to her knees as long as it was getting.

It was in her giant tapestry bag now, shoved underneath her work things so she could sneak a couple of therapeutic rounds in between her classes.

Calvin was finally finished and she said bye distractedly to his moms on her way out, digging her phone out of her bag. Three messages, two from Rachel and — one from Katie.

She made herself read the ones from Rachel first and then swiped on Katie's name.

Dear Eva, can we meet? I really want to talk.

She pulled out her knitting and sat in the car, knitting furiously while she thought. She had heard from Charlie about some pro bono lawyer contacting the shelter from a San Francisco office and helping them, and she just knew it was Eva. But that still didn't explain the weekend at the Lodge.

Or getting more involved with a woman who was leaving for a city over eleven hours away. That way just lay heartbreak.

She looked at the cloud of white fuzz on her lap and groaned. It was way too long for her, she realised. Although it would've looked perfect on Katie. The pale cream setting off her chestnut-brown hair, the long sleeves just right for her elegant frame. She'd gone and made a girlfriend sweater for a woman who wasn't even her girlfriend.

"Okay," she typed back. "I'll meet you at the Spice Cafe this evening."

Katie replied almost immediately. "I'm free now if you are."

Eva flipped through her phone to the calendar even though she already knew the answer. Yes, she had a two-hour gap between classes. There really was no reason to put off being dumped politely.

"See you there in twenty minutes," she sent. Then she gave in and started the ribbing for the bind-off. Maybe she could find some other gorgeous tall dark-haired woman to fall in love with for the sweater.

At the cafe, Katie was waiting at a table near the back, her hair held back in a messy bun. The tendrils that had escaped framed her face in a way that was heartbreakingly adorable. Eva took a deep breath and sat down at the table.

"I got a masala chai," Katie said. "Would you like one too?"

Eva nodded and then went back to feeling tongue-tied. What was there to say. They sat in an uneasy silence until the waitstaff brought over a second steaming cup. It was, Eva was almost disappointed to find out, really good. She knew she'd be avoiding the Spice Cafe from now on.

"I need to explain about the shelter," Katie started. "I had a professional obligation, but I think I found a solution that will help them."

Eva shook her head. "It's alright, Katie," she said. "Charlie sent the news around about the pro bono lawyer from San Francisco. I kinda guessed it was you."

Katie bit her lip and looked down at her steaming cup. "Does everyone in the knitting circle hate me?" she asked in a small voice.

Eva ached to be able to reach out and take Katie's hand, to reassure her. "No, not at all," she said. "I mean, Charlie has some hurt feelings, but he's coming around. And the rest of us," she exhaled, "well, we understand you were in a hard place with your job. We should've given you a chance to explain."

"I quit that job," said Katie.

Now it was Eva's turn to look away. So it was true. Katie had quit her job and would be leaving. "Oh," she said softly. "Oh. Well, I had thought. I mean, you said it was a possibility."

Then Katie was holding her hand out, open across the table. "I got a new job," she said.

"Where?" asked Eva, not quite sure whether she could be able to take what Katie said. "San Francisco? Or further?"

"What, no," said Katie, leaning over the table closer to Eva. "Nearby in Montail county, as a mediator for the district court. It's about a forty-minute commute which means I'd still get to live in St Brigid—"

"You're staying?" asked Eva. "You're not moving to San Francisco?"

"No," said Katie. Her hand still lay open on the tables reaching out to Eva, but Eva hesitated.

"What about the woman from the Lodge?" she asked finally. "I thought, well I heard she was a friend from San Francisco."

"I forget what a small town this is sometimes," Katie said. "That was Alyssa, my best friend from law school. She knocked some sense into my head about finally standing up for myself and quitting."

"But you're not moving to San Francisco with her," Eva asked, needing to hear it for sure, against the slow fizzing hope that was building in her chest, making her throat full and her heart hammer hard against her ribs.

"No," said Katie. "No. I'm staying here. I love St Brigid," she said, and then she took a deep breath and said, "and I'm starting to fall in love with you, Eva."

Eva blinked. She thought she had heard Katie say that she was in love. In love with her. She looked at Katie and saw that same sweet shy smile she'd fallen in love with and her heart felt so full she couldn't breathe for a moment.

"I'm in love with you too," she managed. She put her hand in Katie's outstretched hand and the two of them smiled goofily at each other across the table, fingers tightly interwoven, together.

Eva didn't quite remember how they'd left the cafe, who had paid or whether they'd knocked over anyone in their haste to get back to Katie's apartment. She didn't even have time to say hi to Tomas who tried his best with weaving between their legs to knock them over.

But then they were back in her favourite place in the whole wide world, the bedroom, and Katie was above her, hair fallen loose over her shoulders and that gorgeous mouth saying exactly what she planned to do to Eva pinned under her.

Eva grabbed her hands and kissed the back of her knuckles. "Katie," she said, "I would have moved to find you. I would move anywhere to be with you."

Katie bent down to kiss her, kissing the tiny trickle of tears running from Eva's eyes. "Don't cry," she murmured, "don't cry."

"I'm so happy," Eva said against the warmth of Katie's mouth.

Kisses turned heated and hands started pulling at clothes, Katie holding Eva as something unbearably precious and Eva pressing herself closer, closer to Katie, the two of them wrapped up in each other's arms and passionately reassuring themselves of their love.

"Are you sure?" Eva asked later, after their love-making had dwindled to slow lingering touches and they were buried warm and close under Katie's duvet.

Katie nodded. "I love living here," she said. "I want to be able to build a home with you, and St Brigid feels like our home."

Eva curled up against Katie's chest, twining their hands together. "It does," she said. "But if you ever need to move, Katie Jones, I want you to know, I will move with you."

"And Tomas," said Katie, fighting back a smiling yawn.

"Of course, Tomas," said Eva. "If Tomas wants to move, we'll have to have some serious conversations with him. But I'd go anywhere with you, Katie, my love."

Katie kissed her sleepily. "Then stay in bed with me."

"Always," said Eva.

22

―――――

Katie scanned the crowd, anxiously looking for Alyssa. She was tagging along with Dan, her currently on-again boyfriend, or one of them, for the big re-opening of the shelter. It wasn't a grand affair by San Francisco standards, just lots of homemade goodies and a deeply grateful speech by Charlie's boss to all the people who'd pitched in to help the shelter with the repairs and refurbishments they needed to beat the property development bid.

But there were a couple of very cute dogs sitting obediently on leashes and a whole room full of adorable cats and kittens for everyone to coo over. Katie felt a wave of local pride when she looked around the room. All the knitting circle were there. After lessons ended, they'd agreed to keep meeting and slowly new faces had joined in so The Stitch was a buzzing hub of knitters every Thursday evening.

She smiled and waved at Ruth on the other side who was chatting to Peggy and Milly. She had new friends too, people from work who'd become real friends outside of the office, shared acquaintances with Eva and a couple from the new class she was treating herself to, spinning at The Stitch.

New friends and a new life, she thought, hugging Eva closer to her side in the crowd. Eva slipped an arm around Katie's waist, knowing that crowds made Katie feel a little overwhelmed and gently steered her over to a quiet corner.

"She'll be here soon," she was reassuring Katie when Alyssa and Dan came in the door. They stood out in their sharply tailored suits but Alyssa cut right through the crowd, abandoning Dan to the enthusiastic shelter staff, to give Katie one of her fierce hugs.

"I love what you're wearing," she said. "It's so soft! Like hugging a cloud."

"That's what it's called," said Katie. "Eva designed and made it, the cloud hug sweater." She turned and shared a private smile with Eva. "But I call it the girlfriend sweater."

ACKNOWLEDGMENTS

Thank you for reading **_The Girlfriend Sweater_**! I hope you enjoyed Katie and Eva's sweet and sexy romance in St Brigid!

If you did, I would be very grateful if you'd leave a review on Amazon. Reader reviews make all the difference, so once again, thank you.

Thanks also to Andreea Chidu for sharing the beautiful cover photograph.

The St Brigid Romance series continues in Book #2, **The Bookshop Kiss**.

The Bookshop Kiss

#2 in the St Brigid's Romance Series

When Selma takes a semester to teach in a small sleepy town, she doesn't expect to find her happy ever after. She's only looking for a quiet place to escape the scandal in Chicago.

Delighted to live near a local bookshop, she's even more intrigued by the woman who runs it… and her kisses.

Becca's always been fine with a book and her cats for company. She's not looking for romance until a fiery woman charges into her bookshop to argue about her book display.

Becca's never been lonely before — but she's never had someone like Selma to miss.

As their romantic summer together ends, they have to decide between long-held dreams and new love, between independence and taking a chance with your heart.

The St Brigid series is a small town lesbian contemporary sweet romance series set in the deep woods and charming cafes of the lakeside college town, St Brigid. Each book is a standalone with no cliffhangers - only true love

ABOUT THE AUTHOR

Jenny Parker lives in the woods with her partner, small daughter, four black cats and one very confused dog.

She loves to hear from readers at jenny@jennyparker-books.com

To sign up for new releases, special shorts and occasional recommendations of wonderful lesbian romances, visit her website, **www.jennyparkerbooks.com**